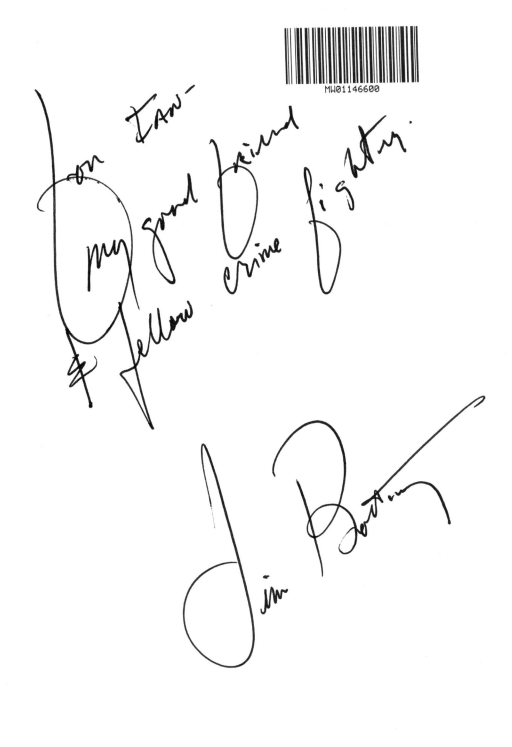

For IAN —
my good friend
& fellow crime fighting.

Jim Barton

River Bottom Rum

A Collection of Stories

James Botting

Library of Congress Control Number: 2012905985
ISBN: Softcover   978-1-4691-9378-6
                 Ebook   978-1-4691-9379-3

This book was printed in the United States of America.

To order additional copies of this book, contact:
Xlibris Corporation
1-888-795-4274
www.Xlibris.com
Orders@xlibris.com
113927

Other Books Published by the Author

Bullets, Bombs and Fast Talk, Twenty Five Years of FBI War Stories, published by Potomac Books, Inc., 2008.

Dedication

This collection of stories is dedicated to all those wannabee writers who stay up late at night cranking out stories hoping to share with the rest of us.

This is also dedicated to the little boy who found a better life in the books of that Denver library a long time ago.

Acknowledgments

The characters and events in this book are fictitious. Any similarity to real persons, living or dead, is coincidental and not intended by the author.

The cover photo and that of the author were taken by Robbin Botting.

None of these stories have been published previously in other media.

Without the encouragement of the following friends these stories would never have left the hard drive of my computer. Stu Abraham, Nick Boone, Dennis Botting, Sam Dorrance, Nancy Glupker, Bob Hamer, Kathleen McChesney, Don McKeon, John Paine, Maria Quijada, John Ripp, Coach Sokolov and Irv Wells.

And of course, a very special thanks to my wife Robbin, who provided the encouragement, support and patience so essential for a struggling writer.

Contents

"Nothing good ever comes from violence."

Martin Luther
German Priest and Scholar

The Early Bird Special

DETECTIVE MAXIMILLIAN SHELBOURNE rammed his Harley into the driveway of Margie's Restaurant, "Home of the Early Bird Special", revved it up a couple times, and then prominently parked in a handicapped space in front. He pulled off his German war helmet and looped it over the handlebars, pealed off his leather gloves and stuffed them in one of the saddle bags. To the unarmed security guard standing on the edge of the parking lot, the huge bearded man with a sleeveless black leather vest, chaps, boots and chains could have been a Neanderthal cave dweller. It never occurred to him to ask for a handicapped permit. Without glancing at the guard, Max clomped into the restaurant and looked around. Mud brown vinyl booths along the wall, red and white checkered oilcloth on the tables crowding the center aisle. Plastic pink roses jammed into small white vases on each table. Electric candles hung on the wall spaced along the booths for nighttime diners. Max felt like he had stepped back fifty years in time.

He noticed Rita and Vic, his backup, had taken their places in a corner where they could observe most of the restaurant. He hesitated and then slid into a booth nearby which would allow them to observe and record the meet. Steam and smoke poured from the kitchen window sending out a meaty smell that permeated the whole restaurant and seemed to stick to the walls. Max guessed there wasn't going to be any sushi on Margie's menu. A Mexican short order cook with a white paper sailor hat and beads of sweat dripping from his chin constantly rang an annoying bell for each order that he readied. Max waited patiently for a waitress and finally waved one over after being ignored for several minutes. He ordered a Budweiser and settled back into the booth to wait. Surrounded by all the senior citizens, he couldn't have been more out of place at a Tupperware party or a baby shower.

At exactly three fifty eight she marched in the front door prodding her path with a three pronged cane like a mine sweeper. She glanced around, then walked up to Max and stopped at his booth.

"Tony Bennett", she said looking directly at him.

"I left my heart in San Francisco", answered Max correctly.

"Thank goodness, you remembered", she said as she carefully collapsed into the seat facing him. "I wasn't sure I'd recognize you even though you did provide a description."

Max fought back a smile. She must be eighty, he thought. This can't be real. "Yeah, well, so what's this all about?"

"You saw my advertisement in the newspaper?"

"Uh-huh", he grunted, "but I'm not sure what you want. I mean, ' . . . an individual experienced in solving personal problems . . .' That could mean anything."

"Yes, well, young man, you see I need some assistance with a personal matter. Something which I can't seem to solve on my own, although God knows I've tried."

"Yeah, OK, so whaddaya talkin' about?"

"Shouldn't we order dinner first? Before we engage in our business discussion. I see you've already started," she said, pointing to his beer bottle. "I hope you're not a drunk. Drunks make mistakes."

Well, you're right about that, lady, thought Max, noticing that her lipstick had been applied without using a mirror.

"Should we introduce ourselves?" she asked pleasantly as if they were on a blind date.

Max laughed. "Lady, names got no place in this business. We're here to talk about a job. What you need and what I can provide. And what it's gonna cost. Now what's this all about?"

She smiled sweetly like a palm reader about to promise someone an early death. She had a small mouth filled with shiny gold molars.

"I want you to kill my husband."

Max blinked behind his sunglasses. He slowly rubbed the mike taped to his chest hoping the scratching would get the attention of Rita and Vic. He stole a quick glance in their direction and received a slight head nod from Rita who tapped her earpiece.

"Now then, I suggest we order first before we get into the details. They have an excellent early bird special here. I prefer the chicken or fish but you look like the meatloaf and potatoes type."

Max looked at her carefully. White female, had to be mid eighties. Couldn't weigh more than a hundred. Neatly attired in an emerald terrycloth pants suit. Sturdy black nun shoes. A red paisley scarf wrapped casually around her neck to hide the turkey wrinkles. Natural white hair, thinning, with the blue tinge. Square red rimmed glasses enlarged twinkling blue eyes. A small diamond wedding ring. Somebody's grandmother.

"Nah, I'm good", Max offered, "But you go ahead and order somethin'."

She waved over the waitress who studied both of them intently. An odd couple. Maybe a wayward son meeting mom for dinner to ask for money. Max hadn't removed his sunglasses and remained an incongruous figure in a restaurant full of retirees who had shuffled in for the early bird special. Wheelchairs, walkers, and oxygen tanks were parked at the various tables like silent companions.

After studying the menu she decided on the seared tuna steak, with a green salad, Italian on the side please, no cilantro, and raspberry tea. Max ordered another beer. After the waitress disappeared she leaned back in her chair and stared at him. She had expected a slick sort of con man. Instead she faced an aging biker trying to look tough.

"Have you done this sort of thing before?"

Realizing the opportunity, Max put on a fierce look and growled, "Look lady, I never talk about my jobs. The less you and I know about each other the better."

It was a worn-out line from an old movie and they both knew it.

"Of course", she smiled.

Max tried to get back on track. "So what's going on with your husband?"

"I need someone to take care of him."

"Take care of him?"

"That's what I said. Take care of him. Get rid of him."

"Life insurance?" probed Max. He couldn't imagine an affair.

"He won't take a bath."

"He won't take a bath?"

"That's what I said. He won't take a bath."

Max thought he heard a snicker from the direction of Rita and Vic.

"He won't . . . take . . . a . . . bath."

"No, several months ago he just announced that he wasn't going to bathe anymore. He said that the human body has natural oils that cleanse it and that he didn't need to take a bath or a shower anymore. He had been reading some holistic literature he received in the mail."

"So he hasn't taken a bath . . ." Max started.

"Not in six months."

"Six months!"

"That's what I said. Six months. And I will not engage in intimate relations with a man who does not bathe. I will not. It's just simply barbarian."

Max looked at her incredulously. The visual of this woman being sexually . . . "OK, lemme get this straight. You want me to kill your husband because he won't take a bath. Is that right?"

"Yes."

"Have you thought about divorce?"

"Divorce?"

"Uh-huh."

"Neither one of us would approve of a divorce," she said with distaste.

"No?"

"No, it would suggest that our marriage has failed. Neither of us could accept that embarrassment. We do have our pride, you know."

Max shook his head.

"Have you thought about another man? I mean, like, gettin' a little somethin' on the side?"

"An affair? My goodness, I could never cheat on Ernie. Never. I respect him too much."

"Respect?"

"That's what I said. I respect him too much."

"But you want him killed?"

"Yes, it appears to be the only solution. But I don't want it to look like an accident. That would embarrass Ernie. As if he had failed in some way. I was thinking, maybe, just a good old mugging on the street. Something appearing random; something he'd have no control over. That way he could go out with pride. His friends would respect him for that."

Max leaned back in his chair, fascinated.

"I brought a photograph for identification purposes. So you could recognize him."

She dug through her purse and pulled out a five by seven color photo. An old man, bald, with huge cataract wraparound sunglasses stood in front of the steps of a small bungalow. He wore Bermuda shorts and a red cardigan sweater with a fat cigar stuck in the corner of his mouth like a snowman. His bird legs accented the size of the man's stomach which suggested that physical fitness was not one of his priorities. A bored bulldog with an enormous red tongue dripping out of the side of his mouth sat patiently beside him.

"That's Ernie", she said with a sly grin, "The one on the left."

Max glanced up at her quickly and snorted at her weak humor.

The waitress returned and delivered her salad and tuna steak. She brought another beer for Max.

"Thought you'd be ready for another," she said pushing her hair back behind her ears and giving him a wide-mouthed smile. She had that tired, single mom working two jobs look. They all like the bad boys, thought Max. He nodded in appreciation but cancelled a smile to stay in character. He unconsciously flexed the faded barbed wire tattoo on his bicep.

"So is there a time frame here?" he asked.

"The sooner the better", she nodded. "You see, I don't know how much time I have left. And there is another gentleman. At our swimming exercise class, we see each other. He seems to be interested."

Max shook his head. "Well, I'm not sure I'm interested."

"What? Why not? Is it the money? How much . . . what is the fee for your services?"

"Look lady, I don't think you can afford me."

She pursed her lips. "I've saved twenty eight hundred dollars, and with my social security check next month, which is three hundred and eighty four dollars, I'll have over three thousand dollars."

Max shook his head, "I don't know . . ."

"Now you listen to me, young man", she shook her finger at him. "You're not going to take me to the cleaners. I read about the Mexican Mafia in the newspaper and it said they'll kill anyone for a thousand dollars. Even less in prison. So three thousand is a good price for this job. And it will be simple because Ernie will be an easy hit. That's what they call it, don't they? A hit?"

They both stopped talking while she waved over the passing waitress and ordered mint chocolate chip ice cream for desert.

Max shrugged. "If I walk away from this one. Then what?"

"Well, then I'll just find someone else", she answered with a flash of anger poking her fork at him. "I thought you were the right man. You bragged about yourself in that letter you sent to my post office box. All that stuff about you carrying out assassinations in Iraq, and South America and Detroit. And now you're getting cold feet. What kind of hit man are you, anyway?"

She paused, and lowered her voice. "And don't think that your letter was the only one I received."

The thought of another letter forced Max to back up. "So where could I find Ernie to do this?"

She leaned back and smiled. "Oh, that will be easy. He's as regular as Monday."

"Huh?"

"He's a tremendous creature of habit. In some ways Ernie has become a very boring man. And then again, after fifty six years, I . . ." she trailed off and took a breath. Her eyes misted just a bit, before she regained her composure.

"He has chemotherapy for his prostate cancer every other Wednesday afternoon at the V.A. hospital and he usually parks in the lot across the street. Here's the address and a description of his car. It's a blue Oldsmobile with a McCain-Palin bumper sticker." She withdrew a note from her purse and shoved it across the table to Max.

"On Saturday mornings", she continued, "He has coffee with his world war two buddies from the Purple Heart Club at the Coffee Bean on the corner of Duluth and Fourteenth Street. And every other Friday night he plays bingo at Immaculate Heart over on Ninth Avenue. You could pick him off at any of those."

"Pick him off?"

"Yes, you know, carry out your assassination."

Max continued to study her, mesmerized, wondering how any district attorney in the free world could possibly convince a jury that this woman was guilty of seriously soliciting the murder of her husband. Especially if she were to testify.

He turned up the heat a little. "You want him to suffer a little? I mean, I could knee cap him first, or maybe use a knife."

"Oh heavens, no. Ernie is a good and decent man. I wouldn't want you to hurt him. I would think some kind of firearm would be best. Kind of like killing a half dead dog that you've accidentally run over with your car. A quick, clean shot to put him out of his misery . . . so to speak."

Max shook his head slowly, disbelieving her diabolical instructions.

She opened her purse, withdrew a fat envelope and pushed it over to him. "Look at this."

Max opened the envelope and looked at several one hundred dollar bills.

"There's twenty eight hundred in there", she said adding the photo of Ernie to the envelope.

Max shrugged, unimpressed. "Look, normally this would easily be a ten thousand dollar job."

"Oh, my goodness", she said with disappointment. "Now that would be a problem. Maybe I should find a guy from the Mexican Mafia. Although I would probably need to hire a Spanish interpreter, don't you think? I mean, to conduct proper negotiations."

Max gave in. "OK, I'll do it for three grand."

"Okey-dokey." She smiled with relief. "Do you offer a senior citizen discount?"

Max was beginning to think he ought to look around for a hidden TV camera; that he was going to be all over YouTube tomorrow.

"You got a pen?"

She opened her purse and dug around before finding one attached to a checkbook with a rubber band. She handed it across the table to Max.

He looked directly at her and hesitated.

When she gave him a subtle nod he scribbled a phone number on a "Home of the Early Bird Special" napkin. When he finished he pushed it over to her and slipped the envelope into his vest pocket.

"Call me at this number when you get the rest of the money."

She smiled and extended her hand. The ugly blue veins stood out like freeways on a map.

Ignoring her hand, Max stood up, dropped a twenty on the table and walked out towards Rita and Vic. When he reached their table, he hesitated.

"Be gentle, and give her a few minutes to finish her ice cream."

Easy Money

"EASY MONEY, PARTNER. Easy money", Ritchie chuckled as he sat behind the wheel working on his sketch of the parking lot. It was the third day in a row they had parked his old oxidized blue El Camino in the shade under the trees and waited for the arrival of the afternoon Wells Fargo armored truck.

"It just don't seem right though, Ritchie", said Bullfrog. "Taking money from these workin' stiffs. Seems like everybody going in there is driving a junker, has got too many kids, or's walkin' with a cane. Some of them cripples even driving a fuckin' golf cart."

Ritchie looked over at his partner and shook his head.

"We ain't robbing them, stupid. We're robbing Wal-Mart. The money belongs to Wal-Mart. And we're really robbing China. Ninety per cent of all the shit in that store was made by a bunch of Chinese political prisoners. If everybody stopped shoppin' at Wal-Mart China would go broke overnight and they'd all go back to their rice paddies. Plus Wal-Mart got insurance which means nobody really loses anything."

Bullfrog looked over at Ritchie and realized how much he admired his intelligence. That's what you got when you hooked up with a white collar con man. Smarts. He and Ritchie had been cellmates for only a couple months when he first got to Folsom, but they had remained friends and often saw each other in the yard. Talked about life outside the wire and how to make a buck in a hurry. And after Bullfrog had done his three and a half years for possession and sale he'd looked up Ritchie after he was released. Ritchie had done only a couple years for a bank fraud scam and had picked up a telemarketing position when he got out. But both were bored. The armored car job had been Ritchie's suggestion. Bullfrog would never have been able to put that together by himself. No, it took a white collar con man like Ritchie with brains to pull off something as big as this.

Ritchie glanced over at Bullfrog and laughed. He even looked like a moron. A walking talking example of reverse Darwinism. Home schooled by a crackhead mother bunking with an alcoholic boyfriend who beat him with the regularity of an unemployed welterweight, Bullfrog was a born loser. Nothing seemed to match, or fit. As if he had been created by a computer like the cops use to make composite drawings of serial rapists. His bald head was egg shaped and lopsided, making you inclined to tilt your head when you talked to him. His ears looked like Spock's and the nostrils were huge and hairy, like a double barreled shotgun pointed at you. Caterpillar eyebrows. And the eyes. He had this thyroid thing going on that made his eyes bulge out. First day at Folsom, one of the other inmates took a look at him and said he looked like a dumb ass bullfrog trying to shit a chicken bone. And the name stuck. Bullfrog.

Except for when he appeared before the parole board. No sir-ree Bob, then he was Mr. Robert B. Bullard, and yes sir, he was very embarrassed and remorseful about his drug use and sales, and no sir, he wasn't going anywhere near that poison again. He was going to become a productive member of society. Yes, sir, they were going to be proud of him. And to his surprise they had bought his bullshit and now here he was sitting in a Wal-Mart parking lot with a big time con man getting ready to make the biggest score of his life. Yes sir, if you're patient enough sometimes good things just fall into your lap.

"So how much ya think we'll score?" asked Bullfrog.

Ritchie stroked his goatee thoughtfully, "Twenty, maybe thirty thousand."

Bullfrog looked over his shoulder and back at Ritchie. "Maybe we oughta hit one of them high end stores, ya know, where Jenna Jameson and all them movie stars go."

Ritchie laughed. "What are you, fuckin' stupid? Those people don't have any money. It's all about plastic. They don't have any cash. They buy a two dollar cup of coffee at Starbucks with a gold plated credit card. No, you idiot, this is the money tree, right here in the midsection of Sam Walton's America."

"O.K., dude," Bullfrog leaned back in the passenger seat and put a foot on the dash. "You're the boss." He decided right then and there he'd leave the rest of the thinking part to Ritchie.

2:10 PM. The Wells Fargo armored truck lumbered into the parking lot and rolled by the old blue El Camino sitting under the trees in front of the parking lot CCTV cameras. It screeched to a stop directly in front of the main door. Four seconds later the door opened and a guard hopped out with a briefcase in his left hand and a gun in his right.

Ritchie licked his fingers and made a notation on his sketch. He had this habit of licking his fingers like a bookie in an old movie.

"See", he muttered, "It's important to keep notes and you gotta be flexible. He was ten minutes early today."

Bullfrog nodded and looked at him with a smile as wide as a slice of watermelon. He was learning from the master. He thought about making his own notes but he wasn't quite sure what to write down.

Three minutes and forty five seconds later the guard reappeared in front of the store. He still carried the briefcase in his left hand and the gun in his right. His head swiveled from right to left as he walked rapidly to the truck. Jittery as a nervous Chihuahua. When the door opened from inside he climbed in and disappeared. Ten seconds later the truck started moving and rolled out of the parking lot. Ritchie made more notes.

"O.K.," Ritchie noted, "We gotta get the jump on him coming out of the store, before he gets to the truck. We have to surprise him, and watch for the second guard inside the truck. You'll probably need to fire a couple shots at the truck to make him keep the door shut."

"Me? I fire at the fuckin' truck?" asked Bullfrog incredulously.

"Yeah, you. See, that ain't my M.O. and I've never done anything like that. You're a street guy. Bigger and badder than me. You got the balls for it, man. Besides, you don't have 'ta shoot anyone; you just gotta convince him to keep the door shut."

Bullfrog slid down in his seat and thought about shooting at an armored truck.

After a couple minutes he turned to Ritchie, "So how do we get the money from the guard?"

"Oh, that's the easy part. I'll wait for him just outside the door and stick a gun in his back when he comes out. I mean, I won't really have a gun, but he'll think I do. See, if I had a gun we could get in a shootout. This way, I'll unload the pepper spray on him, grab his gun and take the briefcase. He won't have a chance. We'll hop in the car you're going to steal tonight, drive over to the other shopping center, switch cars, and we're gone. What could go wrong?"

Bullfrog mulled the plan over for a couple minutes.

"So all I gotta do is shoot at the armored truck and drive the getaway car, right?"

Ritchie nodded. "That's it. You still got a piece, right?"

"Oh yeah, 'course", although he had to think about where he had stashed it. It had been a long time since Bullfrog had carried a gun on one of his dope deals. And it hadn't been fired for years.

"So tell me again Ritchie, how come you ain't gonna have a gun?"

"Don't need one. That way I can't be charged with armed robbery."

"Well, what the hell about me?" asked Bullfrog. "I'm supposed ta shoot at the armored truck. Ain't that armed robbery?"

"Nope. Not if you don't point it or shoot at anyone. You're just shooting at the armored truck which isn't a person. It isn't a person so it can't be a crime victim."

Bullfrog sat silently thinking about why an armored truck couldn't be a crime victim.

He looked over at Ritchie, "You learnt that shit in the law library in the joint, didn't ya?"

Ritchie grinned. "Didn't know I was a fuckin' lawyer, did ya?"

They both laughed.

"O.K., so we're good now, right?" Ritchie looked at Bullfrog. "You know what you gotta do before tomorrow?"

"Yeah, get us a car tonight."

"Right. Nothing fancy, nothing new, nothing red," Ritchie instructed as he pulled up to Bullfrog's apartment building and skidded to a stop.

The huge salmon colored four story monolith squatted on several acres in the stomach of the city and had originally provided Section 8 housing for over a thousand occupants. Forty years later the Pacific Gardens project had become a classic example of urban decay, no longer a favorite of the politicians propped up by governmental funds and support. Burnt out and scheduled for demolition, only the vocal protests and legal actions of a multitude of special interest groups on behalf of the last few remaining tenants had kept the wrecking ball and the bulldozers at bay.

Bullfrog opened the door and the blended stench of garbage and urine wafted into the car without apology. As he started to slide out Ritchie patted him on the shoulder.

"Later, dude. And hey, one more thing . . ." he paused. "You need to start thinking about how to spend all that money tomorrow. Maybe like finding a new pad, man."

Bullfrog laughed. It sure was great working with someone who could figure out all the angles.

The next day shortly after noon Ritchie pulled into the shopping center and slowly scanned the parked cars. He drove down several rows before he heard two short beeps of a car horn. He glanced to his left and saw Ronald Reagan waving at him from a black Buick with a gray primer hood. He found an open space, parked the El Camino and quickly walked over to the Buick. He slid into the passenger seat and glared at Bullfrog.

"Take that mask off, you idiot. Everyone is going to notice you. Whose idea was it to wear a fucking mask?"

Bullfrog looked hurt. "I jus' thought it would be a good idea. Actually, I picked out the Bill Clinton one, but my girlfriend liked Ronald Reagan.

She ain't political or nothin', ya know, she just liked Reagan's hair better."

"Your girlfriend?" Ritchie screamed. "You told your fuckin' girlfriend about the plan?"

"Uh, yeah", Bullfrog gulped, suddenly realizing that might have been a mistake.

"You moron, don't you know a chick will give you up in a goddam minute? The first time you piss 'em off they'll drop a dime on ya."

They both sat for a few minutes without saying anything. Bullfrog fidgeted while Ritchie considered scrapping the plan. The silence finally got to Ritchie.

"So where'd you get this piece of shit?"

"It's a '98. Pulled it out of the Rent-A-Wreck lot on south Broadway last night," Bullfrog said proudly. "Even got the keys. Didn't have to punch the ignition this time."

Ritchie calmed down a bit. "Alright, O.K., let's get over to Wal-Mart."

Minutes later they pulled into the lot. Bullfrog drove around a couple times while Ritchie studied his sketch and finally directed him to a parking place. It was closer to the store than they had ever been which made Bullfrog nervous.

"Just relax", Ritchie reassured him, "This'll go like clockwork."

They had waited twenty minutes when a blue shirted Wal-Mart employee came out and walked up to the car. White guy, in his early twenties. Bullfrog shoved his Ronald Reagan mask under the seat. Ritchie sat up, adjusted his sunglasses, and turned the sketch of the parking lot over on his lap.

"Hey, guys", he leaned a tattooed forearm on the drivers door frame like the highway patrol and almost stuck his head inside Bullfrog's open window.

"Sorry, but this is a loading area for our physically challenged customers and I'll have to ask you to move. That is, unless you have a handicapped placard."

Bullfrog recoiled and looked at Ritchie helplessly.

Ritchie spoke up without looking directly at him, "Yeah, sure, we'll move. Sorry."

He nodded at Bullfrog who turned the ignition key. Nothing happened. Bullfrog turned it again. Nothing. Then he flipped it on and off rapidly several times. Nothing. Ritchie swore quietly. The employee, who had started back towards the store, stopped and turned around.

"Need some help? I can call you a tow, or maybe find some jumper cables."

Suddenly it caught, and Bullfrog pumped the accelerator to blow out the carbs. A huge plume of black smoke belched into the air as he revved it up. Several people walking by looked over at the car. One of them smothered a laugh. Couple of grease ball losers.

Jesus, thought Ritchie, this is a great start. "Got it", he yelled out the window at the blue shirt who turned around and walked back towards the store. "Don't shut this damn thing off again, you fool," he spit at Bullfrog.

1:37 PM. Ritchie checked his watch. They had about twenty five minutes. They used ten to find another space to wait for the armored truck.

"O.K., now," Ritchie reminded Bullfrog, "At about two o'clock I'll walk up to the front of the store and wait for the truck. You sit tight in the car. When you see the guard walk into the store, pull up closer to the truck and get out of the car. Leave it running. DON'T SHUT THE FUCKING THING OFF! Just lean on it, you know, like you're waiting for someone. Just act natural. As soon as the guard comes out of the store, you shoot at the door of the armored truck. I'll pepper spray the guard, take the money and jump in the car. You drive the getaway car out of the parking lot without attracting attention. Got it? Easy money, partner."

Bullfrog mentally went over the plan again and smiled as his confidence grew. Like Ritchie said, what could go wrong?

They both carefully watched the time and a little before two Ritchie got out of the car and walked to the front of the store. He leaned against a trash barrel, lit a smoke and tried to look casual. Bullfrog pulled out his old revolver and looked it over. It had been awhile. He opened the chamber, spun it around a couple times and was examining the bullets when he heard a rumble. The armored truck lumbered up to the front of the store and stopped. The guard jumped out and walked into the store, gun in one hand, briefcase in the other. Just like the plan. Ritchie stiffened and moved closer to the door. Suddenly Bullfrog's mind slipped into neutral. He tried to remember the sequence of the plan, but all he could recall was that he was supposed to shoot at the armored truck. He wished he had kept notes like Richie.

Waiting until his nervousness became unbearable, Bullfrog pulled on his Ronald Reagan mask, opened the car door, and stuck the gun in his waistband. The hammer immediately caught on his shirt. As he tugged at the gun he grazed the cylinder release accidentally dropping the bullets out of the gun. He cursed to himself under the mask as he searched for the bullets scattered on the ground.

"Hi there, Mr. President."

Bullfrog looked up. Two teenage girls were walking by the car. They smiled coyly as if they wanted a presidential ride home and waved as they passed.

Bullfrog straightened the mask so he could see out and looked towards the front of the store. And there he was. Coming right out! The guard with the briefcase in one hand and a gun in the other. And Ritchie right behind him.

All of a sudden Ritchie uncapped the pepper spray and everyone in the immediate vicinity started screaming. The guard went down to one knee, blindly trying to fight off his attacker who was tugging at the briefcase. His gun dropped to the sidewalk and he turned all his attention to hanging on to the briefcase. Bullfrog ran to the rear of the armored truck, pointed his gun at the half open side door and pulled the trigger. It took three clicks for him to remember that he had dropped the bullets back by the car.

"Ritchie", he screamed.

And then, in a fit of desperation and confusing instructions to shoot at the truck, Bullfrog wound up and threw the gun like a ninety mile an hour fast ball at the armored truck. It thumped into the door which slammed back and shut. He ran forward to help Ritchie still pulling at the briefcase which had now ripped open. Within seconds, bills floated in the air mixed with the pepper spray. Handcuffed to his wrist, the guard couldn't have given Ritchie the briefcase if he had wanted to. Seeing the gun on the ground Bullfrog suddenly realized the opportunity. He took a step forward but immediately tripped on the curb hidden by his mask which had slipped to the side of his face. Just as he dove for it a bystander kicked the gun away from him. Sprawled on the sidewalk, he watched helplessly as the gun slid under the armored truck.

Suddenly he was aware of Ritchie yelling, "Go for the car, let's get the hell outa here."

He looked up and saw that the blue shirted employee had joined in the tug of war over the briefcase. Money lay everywhere. Women were screaming and children crying. Bullfrog leaped to his feet and retreated to the old Buick. It was still idling, but rocking back and forth like a dying beast in a grade B sci-fi movie.

Scrambling into the driver's seat, Bullfrog tore off his mask and revved it up to red line in a burst of adrenalin. He heard the door crack open and Ritchie piled in, followed by a cloud of pepper spray. He jammed it into reverse and backed up blindly for twenty yards before he slammed on the brakes and spun around like a moonshiner. They bottomed out as he shot out of the parking lot.

Bullfrog did three straight miles at sixty five with his head hanging out of the window before his eyes stopped burning from the pepper spray. Ritchie slumped down in his seat beside him, tears running down his face uncontrollably, coughing up yellow puky stuff and moaning.

Neither said anything.

When they had put twenty minutes behind the Wal-Mart parking lot Bullfrog pulled off on a side street in a residential area and coasted to a stop at the curb. He shoved it into Park, slumped down and watched the heat waves waffle above the primered hood.

Several minutes passed. Ritchie wiped his nose on his sleeve. "Maybe we need to do a little more work on the plan."

Bullfrog nodded.

Their silence was suddenly shattered by a windstorm, a blinding light drilling into the front windshield, and the voice of God. The Rapture, thought Bullfrog. Jesus Christ, so this is how it ends.

"THIS IS THE POLICE DEPARTMENT. DRIVER, THROW THE CAR KEYS OUT OF THE WINDOW. BOTH OCCUPANTS, RAISE YOUR HANDS."

The police helicopter dropped down in front of them like a spider on a web. Two large bugs stared at them through the Plexiglas bubble. It hovered twenty yards in front of the Buick preventing a frontal escape.

Bullfrog looked into the rearview mirror and noticed flashing red lights from a police cruiser directly behind them. "They're behind us too, Ritchie."

"Holy shit! Where the hell did they come from," screamed Ritchie.

Both officers crouched behind the opened doors of their vehicle with guns pointed at them. One held a microphone.

"DRIVER. THROW OUT THE KEYS AND OPEN THE DOOR."

"What are we gonna do, Ritchie", Bullfrog moaned. "They got us."

Ritchie looked over his shoulder and studied both the cops. "Fuck 'em. Just gimme a minute to figure this out." He twisted around and faced the helicopter in front of them.

"No way, Ritchie," Bullfrog shook his head. "We're never gonna get away."

"DRIVER, THROW THE KEYS OUT THE WINDOW. DO IT AND DO IT NOW!"

The helicopter continued to float in front of them, drifting from one side to the other, kicking up debris and stones from the street which banged off the windshield of the old Buick.

"You should have dumped this piece of shit right after we got away", Ritchie complained to Bullfrog. "That gave 'em time for that helicopter to find us."

"Me? I was just trying to get the hell outa there, Ritchie, with the pepper spray in the car and everything. I forgot about changing cars", Bullfrog tried to explain.

He glanced in the rearview mirror and noticed that one of the cops had replaced his pistol with a shotgun that looked big enough to launch a rocket. He thought about his own gun laying in the street under the armored car back at the Wal-Mart.

"Ritchie, they must think we have guns and stuff."

"Of course they do, you idiot. We just tried to rob an armored truck. That's why they haven't just walked up to the car and asked for your driver's license. I can't believe you, man. Didn't you learn anything in the joint?"

"But we're not, Ritchie, neither of us has a gun. We're not dangerous. And I didn't shoot the armored car either. I just threw the gun at it. And . . . ."

"You what?"

"DRIVER, THROW THE CAR KEYS OUTSIDE THE WINDOW. NOW!"

The frustration of the officer was apparent.

"Ritchie, we gotta surrender, man. It's all over. I'm getting out." Bullfrog threw the car keys out the window and stared to crack open the door.

"Dammit, what'd you do that for," yelled Ritchie trying to make himself heard over the noise of the helicopter.

"Huh?"

"Throw the keys out, you dumb shit. We're stuck. Now we ain't going nowhere."

"Look Ritchie, I thought you had everything figured out, like you had all the angles covered. But now, we're fucked. They caught us. It's over.

Ain't no point just sittin' in the car here." Bullfrog looked at Ritchie and shook his head. "We're goin' back to the joint, partner. Strike two. One more and it's life. We're losers, dude."

"I ain't going back to the joint, man, no fuck-ing way. I'm through with that bullshit."

"Naw, it's over Ritchie, I'm getting out." Bullfrog pushed the door open a little more.

"OK, you chickenshit. "Go ahead, get out and give up. I don't care. I'm through with you. You're a loser."

As Bullfrog opened the door, Ritchie shoved him out into the street. He stumbled down to his knees, regained his balance and quickly stood up.

Turning around to face the officers, Bullfrog started to tell them that he had left the gun back at Wal-Mart when the first bullet caught him in the throat and neatly snipped a carotid artery. The second burrowed into his left kidney and the third punched into the center of his chest. Each hit was a K-5, each fatal without immediate medical attention, the medical examiner would say later. In combination, survival was impossible. Major organ trauma, large volume blood loss, rapid drop in blood pressure. Cardiac arrest, respiratory failure, and finally, brain death.

Bullfrog fell backward into a sitting position and grasped at his throat, stunned at the amount of blood pouring out of his neck. For half a minute his head hung forward, on his chest, gurgling, and then he fell backward and stopped breathing.

Minutes later, Ritchie sat handcuffed in the back seat of the patrol unit, trying not to look at Bullfrog's motionless body lying uncovered in the street. He looked away as a crowd of bystanders from the neighborhood began to form on the curb behind the yellow crime-scene tape. They whispered quietly pointing at him and then at the figure lying in the middle of the street. One of them, a fiftyish woman with an ass the size of New Jersey, wearing a mauve DK jogging suit and holding a small dog, complained to anyone listening.

"Omigod, this is just so wrong. Don't they know what a high end neighborhood this is?"

The helicopter had shut down in the middle of the street and the whirl of the blades had gradually receded. The pilots had exited the Plexiglas bubble and joined the other officers standing by the rear of the Buick. They talked animatedly to each other, getting their stories straight while they waited for the paramedics and a supervisor.

Easy money. Ritchie hung his head.

Rest Stop

THE BEIGE FORD Aerostar finished the long climb up the 405 and merged into I-5 north after coming out of the tunnel. For a Friday morning the freeway was fairly wide open as most of the traffic was southbound into Los Angeles. Wayne leaned back in his seat and tried to get comfortable. He really wanted to be somewhere else, like on the golf course with Vince and Arnie but he'd lost that argument yesterday. Kate's mother had taken a turn for the worse up in Fresno and they'd bundled the family up for the four hour trip. He woke up that morning with something else on his mind and rolled over in bed but Kate had pushed him away and told him to run the dog outside and start the coffee. And pour the kids some cereal. So he'd started the morning frustrated and with a growing anger.

He glanced over at Kate paging through one of her celebrity magazines and checked the kids in the rear view mirror. Nikki was securely belted into her car seat half asleep already. That's the best part of being four thought Wayne, being able to fall asleep anywhere. And Joey, who at six was becoming a serious video gamer. Not the war games of the teenagers yet, but plenty of fascinating animated stuff to keep him occupied. At least for the first half hour.

"You're following too close", said Kate without looking up.

"Whaddya mean", Wayne snorted. "This guy's in the number one lane doing sixty five. That's an illegal act in the state of California."

"I don't care, you're following too close."

Wayne ignored her and continued on. It was a white Mercury with a Nevada license. The Silver State. A visitor to California. He continued a car length behind at sixty five.

"Just pass him, Wayne."

"Nah, I'm gonna make him pull over, he oughta be in the slow lane."

"Well, he isn't. He's probably just somebody's grandpa from Nevada. He doesn't realize he's on the busiest freeway in the world. Just pass him."

Wayne bore down on the Mercury, even closer, a half car length behind, and began flashing his lights. When that failed, he began blowing the horn.

"For Christ's sake, Wayne, just PASS HIM", shouted Kate. "You're scaring all of us."

Wayne gripped the wheel with both hands, ignoring Kate, while he continued to flick the lights and blow the horn.

"Will you please pass him and stop this insanity? Please, Wayne", Kate begged.

"Daddy, what are you doing?" asked Joey from the back seat, suddenly noticing his parents' argument.

Wayne shot a quick glance at Joey in the mirror and then refocused on the Mercury. With a quick move, he slid into the number two lane and tromped on the accelerator.

"Wayne!" yelled Kate. "What are you doing?"

Pulling up alongside the Mercury, he looked over at two senior citizens. The shrunken driver, gripping the wheel at ten and two, was staring intently straight ahead. His wife looked over at Wayne fearfully; her eyes huge. Wayne laughed and flipped her the bird as he pulled away. A few car lengths ahead he jerked back into the lane directly in front of the Mercury and slowed down to sixty. He continued on for close to a mile watching the old man in his rearview mirror. Laughing, he finally pushed it up to seventy five and set the cruise control.

Kate looked at him with astonishment and anger. "Don't you ever do that again, Wayne. That was crazy. You could have killed us all."

He looked at her and laughed. "Get over it, Kate. He was an idiot."

Within a half hour the kids started to get into it over the DVD player. The argument rapidly escalated from words to fighting for possession of the machine. And then slapping at each other.

"Stop it," Kate said twisting around in her seat to face them. "Share it, or I'll take it away from both of you. Joey, let Nikki have it first."

"But it's mine", yelled Joey possessively.

"Dammit", Wayne yelled. "I'm trying to drive. Knock it off Joey. If you don't stop hitting your sister I'll pull over right here and give you a spanking."

Kate looked at him. "Do you realize how stupid that sounds? What happened to a time-out?"

"Time-outs are bullshit. Kids need a good whack every now and then, Kate. Get's their attention. One for correction. A second one to show 'em you didn't make a mistake. And a third one for me, as my old man used to say. We both got our share growing up and look at us. We survived okay."

"That was before we learned more effective child rearing methods than physically beating your child."

"Yeah, and it wasn't called child abuse then either. Slap your kid now and you go to jail," complained Wayne.

"You just have to be reasonable, Wayne."

"Hey, one of the guys in I.T. at the office was getting a divorce and his wife claimed he was physically abusive with the kids. A social worker came to the house to investigate, asked the kid if his old man ever hit him. The kid said yeah he spanked him every now and then. She ended up taking the kid right out of the house. That day. Put him in the foster system for four months before his wife admitted she made it all up. And they billed him fourteen hundred a month for the foster care. Shit like that will make you take hostages, Kate."

"Don't talk that way in front of your children."

Wayne glanced at her sharply, feeling rebuked. "Well, it's true. It happens."

Halfway down the Grapevine Kate winced and looked over at Wayne.

"I have to go potty."

Wayne looked at her. "Why didn't you do that before we left?"

"I did, but I have to go again."

He shook his head in frustration and turned his focus back to driving. Another twenty minutes passed and Kate turned to him.

"OK, look, it's not critical, but I've got to pee. In another five minutes it will be critical."

"OK, OK", Wayne laughed as he pulled off at a Chevron and dropped Kate in front of the restrooms out back. He watched three guys changing the rear tire on a six wheel pickup. They all had that look, like they'd just walked out of the county jail. Wayne shifted in his seat uncomfortably wishing Kate would hurry. They all looked up when she came out of the restroom and eye fucked her as she got back into the van. As he pulled out of the driveway of the station Wayne looked back at them in the rearview mirror. He was relieved to see that they were still working on the tire. Assholes, he thought.

Kate got comfortable in her seat and snapped her seat belt. But somewhere inside her, she had a nagging worry that the reason her bladder was talking to her was not just her morning coffee. She was late, and she'd been late before, but she'd had some nausea lately too. Wayne had publicly declared that their family building days were over. He also made it no secret that he considered raising children a crapshoot and that theirs were still too young to declare a success. No, she thought, if her suspicions were right he wasn't going to be happy with this.

When they hit the bottom of the Grapevine the Aerostar found itself in the middle of six lanes, surrounded by several eighteen wheelers. Feeling like he had just driven into a cave, Wayne tolerated his growing claustrophobia until they hit the I-5 and 99 split. At the first opportunity he slid over into the number one lane cutting in front of a large pickup pulling a boat. It braked hard to give him room.

"Did you see that pickup", Kate asked?

"Yeah, he had enough room."

He hated her criticism of his driving. Her constant bitching felt like poisoned darts. One time coming back from the mountains he got so pissed off he pulled over onto the shoulder, shut off the car and flipped her the keys. He got into the back seat with the kids and told Kate to drive them home. After ten minutes of silence he finally gave up and took the keys back but it was four days before she spoke to him again and that was just to remind him to take out the garbage cans.

Fortunately the pickup didn't fishtail which could have resulted in a major accident. He rapidly ran it up to eighty and then set the cruise control at seventy eight, eight above the speed limit but hopefully not fast enough to attract the highway patrol. They settled down and when the kids nodded off Kate hummed along with an oldies but goodies radio station. Wayne found it annoying but said nothing. It was better than Elvis.

They cruised along in the fast lane setting the pace for those behind until several miles south of Bakersfield when a double bottom gravel truck pulled onto the freeway up ahead. It built up some speed and then pulled into the lane directly in front of the Aerostar to pass another big rig. Wayne grunted, frustrated by having to slow to sixty.

"What the hell does he think he's doing? He needs to move over. Now, dammit."

Kate looked at him. "What is your problem? Slow down. He'll pass that guy and open it up again. Just give him a minute."

Wayne's hands clenched the wheel as he waited for the truck to gradually pass the other. It took a couple miles but seemed like forever to Wayne. Finally, as it gradually merged back into the number two lane the truck dropped a hailstone of gravel which pelted the Aerostar and chipped the windshield. A small spider web appeared in front of Kate.

"Dammit! He chipped the windshield. Sonafabitch", screamed Wayne.

"Wayne, honey, please. We can get it fixed", pleaded Kate.

He pulled alongside the gravel truck matching his speed but was unable to see the driver.

"Flip him off, Kate. No, tell him to pull over. Dammit! Tell him to pull over." He started to lower Kate's window but she immediately rolled it back up.

"Stop it, Wayne."

He veered back and forth towards the truck trying to draw the attention of the driver.

"Wayne, please, stop it. STOP IT! It's not important", screamed Kate. "You're going to get us killed."

With both of them screaming at each other, Nikki started to cry. Joey kept asking "What's the matter, daddy? What's the matter?"

Kate refused to roll down her window and begged Wayne to stop. Several minutes passed before he finally gave up and sped ahead of the truck. Neither said anything for several miles as they drifted through miles of dusty vineyards.

Kate wiped away tears and looked over at Wayne. "What the hell is wrong with you?"

He stared straight ahead with his jaw clenched.

An uncomfortable silence developed between the two of them as the Aerostar continued north on the 99 through the Central Valley like a blood clot slowly making its way through an artery. Past one municipal road kill after another; financially broken agricultural communities showing their ass to the travelers passing through the guts of their city behind tinted windows in air conditioned late model SUVs. Backyards with dead washing machines, junkyards piled high with calcifying vehicles, deserted shopping centers and fallow pastures. Half built housing developments abandoned overnight as if they were radioactive. The Salad Bowl of America had given up trying to hide its economic failures long ago, thought Wayne.

Kate pointed to the "Rest Stop" sign alongside the freeway. "Let's take advantage of that and give the kids a chance to stretch."

Wayne shrugged. "Whatever." By now he didn't care if they ever got to Fresno.

He pulled the Aerostar into the exit lane and cruised into the rest stop parking in front of a drinking fountain. He opened the side doors freeing Joey while Kate unbuckled Nikki's car seat.

The place was the typical interstate rest stop, designed with the same purpose as a drive through restaurant. Minimum loss of travel time. Do your thing and get back on the road. Dirty restrooms with an inch of water on the floor; doors removed on the men's commode stalls to discourage public display of illegal sex acts; a coke machine encased in a steel cage as if it held something of value; a large California map behind glass for protection from the elements; a separate area for truck parking; and of course, an animal recreational area. The larger truck stops that offered petrol and mechanical services were often small communities which offered additional non-taxed services. Cheap drugs, a ten minute love affair in the cab of a truck, and bargain prices for merchandise that had fallen off a tailgate. This one offered restroom services only and was named for a local political hack who had apparently decided that it was better to have a rest stop named after him than nothing. It had probably all started with some guy named Andy Gump.

The four of them walked towards the rest rooms and separated as they neared them. Kate took Nikki to the women's building and Joey followed Wayne. In the rear of the building there was a double entry and exit door to the restrooms. Joey hesitated and stopped to watch an older couple out back playing Frisbee with a Jack Russell terrier while Wayne went inside ahead.

A few minutes later Wayne came out and looked around for Joey. The couple with the Jack Russell had disappeared. He walked around the corner of the building and ran into Kate and Nikki.

"Where's Joey"? Wayne asked.

"I don't know. He was with you".

"No, he's not."

"I thought you had him. He was with you."

Wayne turned around and walked back into the restroom. He looked into each stall. They all were empty. He ran back outside and rejoined Kate.

"I don't know where he is," he yelled. "We've got to find him. Go check in the women's restroom. And check every stall. I'll check the car."

Wayne ran around the men's room building and over to the van parked in front. He checked the doors, found them locked, and no sight of Joey. Panic began to set in and he felt his heart pounding. Then he remembered the old couple with the Jack Russell terrier. With a shout to himself he ran over to the dog run area searching for the couple.

He ran up to a woman holding a black Lab on a leash.

"Have you seen a six year old boy? Wearing a blue Dodgers windbreaker. Have you?"

She shook her head and turned back to her dog walking in circles. A truck driver wearing a red Pendleton shirt with a white teacup Poodle under his arm crawled out of his cab and headed towards Wayne. The rest of the dog area was deserted.

"JOEY, JOEY", Wayne starting screaming at the top of his voice while wandering in circles. "JOEY. JOEY. JOEY."

He ran back to the restrooms frantically calling Joey's name for a couple minutes before running into Kate and Nikki in the front of the rest stop.

"Wayne. Where is he? I thought he was with you," she screamed. "Omigod", she cried. "This isn't happening. We need to call 9-1-1." Seeing her mother cry, Nikki started wailing.

"Shut up Nikki. Just shut up", yelled Wayne. "I gotta think."

"We need to call the cops, Wayne", begged Kate. "Omigod. Where is he? Call 9-1-1."

"9-1-1 is no help", yelled Wayne. "They're an hour from here. No, we've got to find him. He's around here somewhere. Maybe he's hiding, playing games. Stay right here, by the restrooms, in case he comes back. I'll recheck them." With that he ran off frantically calling Joey's name.

Wayne headed back into the men's room and searched again, checking all the stalls again. No Joey.

Once outside, he headed over to the women's room and ran inside. Just a row of stalls. He quickly kicked in the doors and found the fourth occupied. He jumped up and peered into the stall.

"You pervert", screamed the surprised occupant. "Get the hell outta here or I'm callin' the cops."

Wayne didn't take time to answer as he ran back outside.

His thoughts went back to the couple with the Jack Russell terrier. With his heart pounding, Wayne felt like he was having a heart attack. Disregarding the chest pains, he ran over to the dog run and the cars parked in that area. He ran from each car to the next, asking everyone he found if they had seen Joey. One said he thought he saw a kid with an older couple around the dog area, but he didn't see what kind of car they were driving. Screaming with frustration and yelling Joey's name, Wayne ran back to the road and watched the cars. I've got to stop those cars, he thought. He's got to be in one of them.

Park ranger Peggy McIntosh, chestnut hair, freckle faced and with two weeks experience working solo, drove her mint green pickup into the rest stop and noticed a man standing in the middle of the road stopping traffic. He held his hand up and then stuck his head in the window of the car he had motioned over. As she drove closer, he looked up, mouthed something she couldn't read, and immediately headed towards her on a dead run.

She pulled the pickup into an empty space and opened the door just as the man reached her.

"I think my kid's been kidnapped and we've got to stop these cars. He may be in one of them. His name is Joey and he's wearing a blue Dodgers windbreaker. Help me."

"Now hold on, sir. Just a minute", she said adjusting her Smoky Bear hat subconsciously to assert her authority. "Why do you think he's in one of those cars?"

"Because he isn't anywhere else. C'mon, we're wasting time. Please. Help us. C'mon ".

Wayne grabbed her arm which she quickly shook off. She looked at him carefully, wondering if he were a crazy. Disheveled hair, beads of sweat popping out on his forehead. Drunk, doped up? Maybe a parental custody dispute. Then she looked in his eyes and read the panic. No, she thought, this man's hysteria is real and he's unraveling right in front of me. And his kid's probably asleep in the back seat of the car.

"OK, let's have a look. I need to check out your car first though. Make sure he's not there." McIntosh remembered her academy training regarding lost kids. Most are found within a quarter mile of where they were last seen. She also remembered that three fourths of those kidnapped are killed within the first two hours by the kidnapper. After sexual assault. Rapid response was essential for recovery.

Wayne gritted his teeth. "I already checked the car. He's not there."

"I'm sorry, sir. But I've got to check the car first."

"Dammit, we're wasting time." He dug in his pocket and threw her the keys. "It's the beige Aerostar over there", he said, pointing to the van.

He broke into a run back to the road and groaned as he watched passenger cars merging with the trucks departing the rest stop.

A few minutes later the ranger pulled alongside Wayne in her pickup. She rolled down the window and handed him his car keys.

"He's not back at the car," she yelled as she made a sharp left and parked her pickup diagonally across the road. She turned on the blinking red light bar on the top of the cab and jumped out holding a radio.

Within minutes the cars began to back up at the exit, with drivers wondering what sort of emergency had occurred. But the blinking red light and the official presence of the uniformed ranger with a gun and a badge encouraged them to begin forming a line. One by one they crawled towards Wayne and the ranger who conducted a quick inspection of each of the vehicles. They had searched several cars before Wayne realized that he had forgotten the truckers leaving from the rear of the rest stop. And how easy it would be to hide a small boy in one of those huge truck cabs.

"Dammit", he yelled at the ranger. "I forgot about the trucks. Can you go over to the truck area and stop them. He could be there also. Please", he begged.

She looked over at him, hesitating.

He pushed his hair back from his sweaty face with both hands and begged her. "Please."

"Sir, I've radioed the highway patrol for assistance."

"But they won't be here for an hour," moaned Wayne.

"Well, they're coming code three; we'll just have to hope for the best". She hesitated.

"But OK. I'll go over to the trucks."

Without a word Wayne turned his attention back to the line of idling cars which was growing. A large black Mercedes with tinted windows driven by a middle aged black man followed by a Ford Explorer with a young couple and camping gear strapped down to the roof rack. Behind them, an older silver four door with an elderly couple, a young girl at the wheel of a red pickup coughing diesel fumes, and a beat up green Honda driven by a guy with a baseball hat. The last one in line was some kind of van which looked full of people, field workers maybe.

Wayne approached the black Mercedes and hurried up to the driver's window which slid down slowly.

"I've lost my six year old boy and we're just checking everyone leaving the rest stop. He may be playing hide and seek. Please let me look inside your car."

The driver, dressed in a dark suit and white shirt, got out and motioned to Wayne. "Be my guest", he said with a cautious smile. He left the door open and popped the trunk.

Wayne gave the car a quick once over and waved him on.

The Ford Explorer pulled up with the two kids inside. Wayne needed only a cursory inspection to satisfy him.

"Hope you find him, mister", the girl yelled out the passenger side window as they drove off.

Kate suddenly came running up with Nikki in tow. "Where is he? Oh, Wayne, where is he? I saw the park ranger over at the truck area. Omigod! Really? This isn't happening."

She looked around frantically screaming, "JOEY, JOEY, where are you?" Her bottom lip quivered uncontrollably. Tears glistened on her cheeks.

"Help me check these cars", Wayne yelled. He knew he was losing time. And the opportunity. But he didn't know what else to do. If Joey wasn't playing games and hiding somewhere in the rest area, then he had to be in one of these cars.

The silver four door with the old couple pulled forward to Wayne and stopped.

"What the hell's going on here?" growled the driver, a portly white guy about seventy with a Santa Claus beard. His wife was as large as him. Together they filled the entire front seat of the car.

Wayne locked eyes with the driver. "I'm looking for my boy, he's lost. We're checking all the cars to see if they've seen him."

"What'd he look like?"

"He's six, wearing a blue Dodgers windbreaker. His name is Joey."

"Well, we ain't seen him", wheezed the man. "Get outa the way. We're gettin' out of here."

"Mind if I take a look in your back seat"? asked Wayne. The rear seat was suspiciously piled high with clothes and boxes and could have hidden three or four little boys.

"What the hell you talking about, boy, you ain't searchin' my car. You ain't no cop. You got no right."

Wayne grabbed the door handle and pulled the door open.

"You hiding something mister?"

Suddenly he recalled Joey watching the old couple with the Jack Russell terrier. "You got a dog in there?"

"Who you callin' a dog, asshole", the driver cursed as he pulled his large frame out of the car. He stood up straight and came right at Wayne. He aimed a huge right at Wayne's head but he saw it coming and pulled back. As he came around, Wayne pounded his fist into the huge stomach he left exposed and the air whooshed out. He staggered back against the car, regained his balance and the fight was on.

The line of cars waiting continued to grow as the two men fought in the street. A couple impatient drivers blew their horns. As Wayne and Santa continued to battle, the others began to inch off to the side and pass the fight. No one stopped. The young girl in the red pickup knew the danger of hanging around a fight and punched the truck past them. The next in line, the green Honda, had pulled to the right as if to make a U-turn, but then suddenly straightened out and slowly drove past hugging the lane to the left. The driver stared straight ahead ignoring the two men wrestling around. The van full of people with their faces pushed against the windows slowly crept by. It was followed by an elderly couple in a silver Lexus who stared out the windows fearfully.

Kate stood at the side of the car screaming.

"Stop it, Wayne. Stop. Please. Enough. Wayne, please stop it."

Wayne continued to pound away at the old man. When he finally went down he kicked him a few times before standing back to survey the damage. Kate ran up and pushed him away from the man who lay groaning in the street.

"Please, Wayne. Stop. Leave him alone."

He stood there half grinning, smugly satisfied with himself, ignoring the screams of Santa's wife who had run to his side and knelt beside him. As an angry adolescent Wayne had solved a lot of problems with his fists and he felt the satisfaction coming back.

He took a couple deep breaths before leaning inside the driver's seat. He pulled the keys from the ignition and walked to the back of the car to open the trunk. Hearing a muffled whine, he quickly popped the lock, opened the trunk and there, in a small wire cage, was the Jack Russell terrier. Aside from two large feed bags and the dog, the rest of the trunk was empty.

At the north end of the rest stop, the old green Honda picked up speed and gradually merged back onto the freeway. The driver intently scanned the rear view mirror, tugged at his baseball hat and put on a pair of sunglasses. He looked down at the small boy with tears in his eyes and his wrists wrapped in duct tape lying on the floor of the passenger side.

"What's your name, son?"

The Box

I T HAPPENED ON a day when God had gone home early or was more involved with things going on in Fallujah. She had spent a couple afternoon hours in her small garden, nurturing the new seedlings, watering her roses and just enjoying being outside with Daisy, her elderly Beagle, for a change. She was recovering from a recent surgery and as the sun gradually sunk away and the air took on a chill she retreated to her well worn easy chair in front of the TV. And it was then, they guessed, that he slipped in the unlocked back door and confronted her. He beat her senseless with a blunt object they never found and he strangled her with her bra. And he raped her.

"A fucking monster", said one of the detectives. "I mean, who would rape a ninety four year old woman?"

"Well, raping a ninety year old sure ain't about sex", swore another. "We're talking one very angry pervert."

It wasn't until the next morning that her son-in-law found her. He came over to drop off a prescription and opened the front door with his own key. His first clue was that Daisy failed to bark and jump up on him as he came in the door. The second was seeing her lying on the floor, legs splayed apart, nude from the waist down. He didn't even bother to check her pulse before running back outside to call 9-1-1. The first black and white patrol unit arrived seven minutes later and it started. The homicide investigation.

Four days later detectives Nick Florentino and Willard Carrington stood in the homicide squad work bay watching him on a monitor. He was wearing an old pair of jeans and a dark green vinyl windbreaker with the sleeves pushed up to the elbow. Both forearms encased in tattoos. And a black baseball hat with "Mustang Liquor" lettering. He sat comfortably waiting for them. There was no suggestion of worry, anxiety or guilt. He could have been slouched in the local DMV office waiting for his number to be called.

"What do you think?" asked Carrington.

Nick shook his head, "He looks pretty cool, Will".

"Let me try him first, just to get him warmed up, OK?" asked Will.

Nick grinned, "Go get 'im Boo."

He knew that Will would insist on having the first, as well as the last, shot at him. He had honed his interrogation skills well over the years listening to the child molesting monster claim that the little five year old girl was sexy and had really come on to him first. The gang banger defensively explaining how he had to put two rounds from a .45 automatic between the eyes of a kid he'd grown up with. Mutha-fucka dissed me, he'd said, by walking on the wrong side of the street in his hood. And the husband calmly recounting that after working sixteen straight hours on the line at the factory when he came home he deserved something better than a cold slice of leftover meatloaf. And so to register his complaint he picked up one of her Rachael Ray boning knives and jammed it up to the hilt into her stomach while she stood there leaning against the stove with her arms crossed over her chest and that smirk on her face. Will had an amazing ability to just sit there and listen to the evil, nodding slightly every now and then as if understanding and in agreement, while they gradually spilled their guilty guts on the floor in front of him.

It was all videotaped and played in court for the jury. And when they filed out shaking their heads they took just enough time to stop by the restroom and then elect a foreman to take a vote before they returned to deliver the guilty verdict. Yes, he loved the cat and mouse game. The psychological challenge of poking around inside the mind of a suspect and sucking out a confession. Emerging technology had brought a number of improvements to criminal investigation—DNA of course, and AFIS, the automated fingerprint identification system, trace evidence forensics, voice analysis and computer imaging of ballistic trajectory—but the heart of the investigation will always remain the interrogation of the suspect. Getting him to loosen up and start talking, cracking open that door to the secrets, squeezing out some admission of guilt, gradually realizing the futility of denial, and finally belching that cathartic confession. Yes, Will Carrington lived for the interrogation.

Carrington walked down the hall and opened the door to the box.

Eight by ten feet, four walls and a low ceiling designed to encourage claustrophobia. A single steel windowless door which hung heavy. It was furnished with a small rectangular table covered with chipped Formica and three armless steel chairs. Some had a set of handcuffs chained to the leg of the table which provided one cuff for the suspect. This one didn't. The chairs were arranged so that two of them faced a single chair reserved for the suspect which was pushed back against the wall. There was no carpet, no pictures of the police chief or whales leaping out of the ocean, and no friendly reading lamps. Florescent tubes in the ceiling provided minimal lighting and a constant hum which could become annoying while the occupants silently considered their next words. Fisheye camera lens were installed in the false fire alarm in the ceiling and the light switch alongside the door. Both were focused on the chair in the corner and fed the activity in the room to a recorder and video monitors in several locations in detective headquarters. The soundproofed walls were painted a neutral Navaho white as if to suggest objectivity to the adversaries. Carrington could remember in a different era holes the shape and size of a head in the drywall and blood on the walls in some of the old stations. And the smell. A faint mixture of stale sweat and some kind of cleaning solvent. Each box had its own personal history of the unfathomable violence people do to others and the amazing excuses and explanations they offer. Secrets and lies, admissions and confessions, compelled, cajoled, coerced and manipulated through interrogation. Years in prison, life without parole, the gas chamber and the needle, are bartered away in minutes—the box becoming a silent witness and repository for it all.

He looked up at Carrington quickly, somewhat startled, and watched him pull up a chair.

"Hi", said Carrington, "I'm detective Willard Carrington. I need to talk to you. But before I do I need to advise you of your rights. I'm going to read this card to you and then I need you to tell me that you understand all these statements and that you are still willing to talk to me. And of course, you are not under arrest and you are free to leave at any time. You can walk out that door right there. OK?"

He stared at him but said nothing. Then he coughed. A deep, throaty, fluid filled sickening cough that made Carrington want to run. It was a cough that could get him thrown out of an Oakland Raiders football game.

Carrington looked at him intently and hesitated. "OK? So let me read this form."

"You have the right to remain silent. Anything you say can and will be used against you in a court of law. You have the right to an attorney and to have him with you during this questioning . . ." Carrington eventually finished and looked up at him for a response.

"OK, sure, so what's this all about," he asked as he signed the waiver. "I haven't done nothin'."

He leaned back in the chair, crossed his legs comfortably and looked up.

Carrington hesitated, considering an attempt to go after a little background information initially to develop a little rapport and get a feel for him. But then he decided to just jump right in.

"We're conducting a homicide investigation," he answered, "And we're talking to a number of people hoping to find someone who may be able to help us." There, he thought, that's pretty innocuous.

"Homicide? So you think I killed someone?"

Carrington recoiled. Whoa, right in my face. From the gitgo.

"No, we're just talking to a lot of people", he deadpanned. "You never know when you may have something that could help. You could have a piece of the puzzle."

"So what's the puzzle?" he asked. He had deep set watery eyes, milky, like half cooked poached eggs.

"We understand you were doing some work in the vicinity of St. Charles and Third Street the last couple days. Some painting."

"Yeah, I was. So what? Who got killed?"

Carrington hesitated. There was no deflection. The guy kept bringing him right back on line. C'mon, accuse me, he seemed to be saying.

"A woman who lived on St. Charles was killed four days ago."

"So you think I killed her?" he asked. Another fastball right back at him.

OK, thought Carrington, take this, asshole . . .

"Did you?"

"I didn't kill anyone, man. Why do you think I did it?"

Again, right back on point. All designed to flush out the facts of the crime. He had him going. Backpedaling already. Carrington felt his control of the interview slipping.

This guy's pretty good, thought Nick watching on the monitor.

Inside Carrington regained his composure. "Look, we're just talking to everyone in the area and you were around so . . . that's why you're here. We just want to know if you saw or heard anything that might help us."

"Saw or heard what? What am I supposed to have seen or heard?"

Carrington hesitated, momentarily stunned.

He coughed again, right at Carrington who leaned to the side in an effort to dodge the bag of toxic air coming at him like a wrong way driver on the freeway. "You really oughta do something about that."

He nodded. "Yeah, I can't seem to shake it." He paused, "So am I under arrest?"

"No, this is just an interview; you're free to leave anytime you want, like I told you."

"OK," he paused, "So why'd you advise me of my rights?"

Carrington stiffened. "Cuz everyone's got rights, you know. It's just a formality."

"Well, I'm just wondering, like . . . ah . . . how can I be of some help? I don't want you to think I had anything to do with this."

He leaned forward in a display of sincerity, but he failed to disguise an underlying curiosity that Carrington sensed would keep him from walking out the door and probably saving his ass.

"OK, thanks, well . . . look . . . give me a minute", muttered Carrington, as he walked out of the box.

The door swung shut and he startled slightly as the lock clanged. Watching on the monitor, Nick noticed his reaction. Will walked into the hallway shaking his head. He accepted a cup of coffee and took a cigarette from Nick. He lit it and took a long drag as they walked outside to the rear parking lot.

"This prick is really starting to piss me off," Will complained. "He's just demanding that we accuse him, which means we've got to give up something. And I'm not ready for that. Not yet."

"Yeah, I'm just waiting for fingerprints and the DNA shit to come up", said Nick. "He's gotta be wondering about that. If he's the guy, and he used a condom, he knows there probably isn't any semen. So we can't bullshit about that. And the only blood we got is most likely from the victim and the dog. He may be worried about having left some prints somewhere though. Or hair. He might've worn gloves, but for some reason I doubt it. He's probably feeling pretty confident right now."

"Yeah, too confident to lawyer up," snorted Will. "Or too stupid."

"Let him run his mouth for awhile", suggested Nick. "He might surprise us and step on his dick. I'll do a little more computer work on him, priors and M.O.'s, and I'm still waiting for the phone records from the victim's cell. They've got the numbers called, but they haven't ID'ed all the subscribers yet. The search warrant may take awhile."

It had been a long hour of the same shit. He hadn't given them anything but he hadn't walked out or lawyered up yet either. It wasn't a game for him though, because he was truly worried. That was apparent. He was full of CYA answers, " . . . maybe, to the best of my knowledge, if I can remember it right, I'm not sure, I could be wrong, but . . ."

He had to be careful with his alibi though. He knew they'd work that over pretty good. But they couldn't satisfy his curiosity. And that kept him in the box waiting for one of them to slip up and drop some little factual nugget. Forensics maybe, or better yet, identify a witness. Nick had taken a shot at him but only pissed him off when his questioning turned to his prior criminal convictions. He didn't want to talk about that stuff. "You tell me", he'd said flippantly. While Nick sparred with him, Will wandered back to his cubicle and collapsed in his chair.

The cube was filled with the usual cop stuff. Wanted posters, subpoenas, composite drawings stuck on a cork board. The weekend standby-duty schedule. A large calendar mat on the desk filled with handwritten notes and drawings, mostly unreadable, penned during endless telephone conversations. Hung on the side of the wall was a picture of two kids sitting on ponies looking directly at the camera. The girl looked happy and was waving her hand; her younger brother hidden under a helmet too large for him looked about to cry. He had kept a framed black and white photo of Belinda and him kissing on the beach at Cancun on their honeymoon, but he'd taken it down the day she filed the divorce petition. He referred to her as the plaintiff now. Will took a deep breath and leaned back.

Directly in front of him at eye level on the cubicle wall was a series of photos of a young girl. Blonde, freckles, with a toothy smile. Seven in a row from left to right. She grew progressively older with each photo, the freckles receded, and she had added glasses in the last two. They were the class photos of Lindsey Becker taken from the first to the seventh grade and represented the years that Lindsey had been molested by her father. From six to twelve. It had started with fondling, progressed to sharing oral sex and then intercourse at ten. It had all ended when she attended a slumber party with several of her girlfriends and they were playing the "secrets and lies" game. Their first boyfriend, their first kiss, their first period. Young girl secrets. And when it came time for Lindsey's turn, she stunned them all into silence when she told them what her father had been doing to her for the last seven years. And then the next day one of them had told her mother and she had told her husband and someone called the cops, and the complaint ended up on Will's desk.

One of the precinct detectives had initially interviewed Lindsey and her mother before the case had been kicked downtown to Will, who was assigned to the sex crimes task force at the time. After reading the interview of Lindsey, Will had called her father and arranged for him to come down to headquarters for an interview. Yes sir, of course, he'd said. Must be some misunderstanding. I'll be there in an hour.

But he wasn't, and instead he'd gone directly home and pulled out that old military Colt .45 automatic he kept in the closet and shot Lindsey in the head and her mother in the face when she tried to intervene, and then turned the gun on himself. Well, sort of. He could have done everyone a favor and shot himself in the head, but instead he'd put one in his chest. The neighbors had heard the gunshots and called 9-1-1 and the paramedics and the ER docs had saved his life. Will was transferred over to homicide and put the case together. He was convicted of two counts of first degree and the only reason he got double life without parole instead of the needle was that he was paralyzed from the chest down.

Will's eyes swept over the series of photos of the smiling young girl and he remembered the horrific crime scene at the house. You poor little angel, he thought. After a life of hell, just when you thought you'd been rescued this bastard snuffed out your life. That's also when Will had started trading his evening workouts in the department gym for blood pressure medication and Grey Goose.

Will sucked down the rest of his coffee, kicked back his chair and returned to the box. He caught Nick walking out swearing to himself. After a brief conversation Will pulled the door open and walked back in.

He looked up at Carrington with interest, as if expecting an announcement of some kind.

He was disappointed.

"So tell me again what you were doing over there on St. Charles," Carrington asked.

"Painting the outside of that warehouse", he responded with irritation. "Look, man, I told you that, which is the reason I'm here today, right?"

"Yes. And you were telling me that after work you drove to a bar down on Ninth Street, you can't remember the name, had a couple beers with nobody in particular, and then you drove home. Right? Is there anyone who can vouch for that? I mean, if we go to that bar and show your picture around is anybody going to recognize you? How about the bartender?"

"Look, I don't go around asking people to remember me. Or vouch for me 'cuz the cops are probably going to stop by in a couple days and accuse me of committing murder. I mean, like I can't remember what I did every minute of my life. Can you describe every place you went to in the last couple days? Gimme a break, man. I had a couple beers and went home. Big fucking deal. So when did this murder happen?"

Carrington studied him for a moment, looking for a facial crack in his confidence. Nothing showed. The guy was just begging for an accusation in an effort to learn what they had. He considered showing him a photo of the victim, but figured he'd just brush it off. He wasn't ready to show him a picture of his violent handiwork. Not yet.

"The deceased lived in the house next to the warehouse. You worked right next door for three days in a row. You had the opportunity." Carrington paused, "And maybe the inclination. You've got two prior convictions for forcible rape. Two strikes. You're a registered sex offender. All of which makes you pretty interesting."

He recoiled and snapped back, "I was wondering when you'd throw that shit at me. Hey look, I did my fucking time for society. Hard fucking time. Hey, check this out, man."

He shut one eye and then the other, displaying a tattoo on each eyelid; "hard" on the right, "time." on the left. Carrington shuddered inwardly.

"That's a reminder for me every day. It wasn't easy, man. Twelve fucking years. Fightin' everyday at Folsom, Pelican Bay where I almost lost my mind, and Wasco with a bunch of child molesters. And five more years in the snake pit at Atascadero before I could convince them shrinks to give me a chance back in the world. But that isn't good enough for you, is it? No, now you're trying to hang this one on me. Well, I didn't kill that old woman. I swear on my mother's grave. I didn't kill nobody. I swear to God."

He coughed again and wiped the spittle off with the back of his hand.

Nick smiled at the monitor and hoped Will had caught it. The psychological barrier had cracked a bit.

"Did I say she was an old woman", Will asked, pushing back a smirk.

"Huh, whaddya mean", he said. His eyes widened a bit. Oh, oh. Shit.

"You said you didn't kill that old woman. I didn't tell you she was an old woman. Why would you think the victim was an old woman?"

He looked at Carrington, his eyes blinking more now, trying to keep up with the speed of his brain waves. He realized the water was beginning to rise around him.

"Why, I just got the impression that she was old. I don't know. Didn't you say she . . . how old was she, anyway?" Another attempt to make the detective give up something.

Carrington brushed the question aside.

"Were you ever inside the house?"

"Who, me?"

"Yeah, you."

"Inside the house?"

"Yeah, inside the house."

"Which house?"

"Jesus, . . . c'mon. The one on St. Charles where the deceased lived."

Carrington watched him closely thinking how he'd really like to stab him in the eye.

He hesitated. "I'm not sure I know exactly what house you're talking about." He fought off the subtle suggestion that he admit a familiarity of it. This guy's pretty good, he thought, trying to trip me up.

"The gray one, with the white trim." Carrington pushed down a growing anger. "Has a chain link fence in front. The one right next to the warehouse you were painting."

Here we go again, thought Carrington. Everybody lies. Everybody. Even when they don't have to. Put two of these assholes in a room with a hammer and one of them will end up dead. We live in a fucked up world of human conflict and violence, he always said.

"Oh, that one", he scratched at his three day beard as if trying to recall. He desperately wanted to deny that he was ever inside the house, but he had been and he wondered what they had found of his inside.

Carrington watched his brain shifting into high gear.

Did I leave something inside there, he wondered. They can't have any semen because I used a condom. She didn't pull any hair out because she didn't resist. Did she scratch me with her fingernails leaving some skin or blood? No, she hadn't fought back at all. What could they have? If they had something from inside, he was going to have to explain why he was in the house. He licked his lips and looked up.

"Maybe. I don't remember. I mean . . . I don't know."

Better to admit something but remain vague. If they came up with anything, he'd be able to say it must have been when he . . . .

"Yeah, well I did return her dog to her one day. An ankle biter, got out, running in the street, and I caught it and brought it back to her. Rang the door bell, no, maybe knocked on the door [maybe they do have fingerprints from the door], can't remember, and kinda stood in the doorway, just talked to her a couple minutes. About dogs, you know. She thanked me for bringing the dog back. That's all."

Will smiled. "So you do know which house we're talking about?"

"Yeah, I guess so. I mean. If that's the right one. The one you been talkin' about."

Nick smiled at the monitor. He's struggling now. The victim's daughter had told them that the Beagle never went anywhere except the backyard. In fact it was afraid of the traffic in front of the house. He's sinking, he thought. You lying sack of shit. You're drowning right here in front of us.

Carrington was getting warmed up.

"So you've been inside the house then", he asked for confirmation. "Is that right?" He needed to lock him into being inside the house.

"Look, I don't like the way this conversation is going. I mean, like I'm getting the impression that you think I might be the one killed her, and I'd never do anything like that. I've had about enough of this bullshit."

He was starting to feel a little uneasy and he didn't like this large black man. It wasn't just his menacing muscular build, and that he looked like the former linebacker that he was. But he found Carrington's questioning more threatening. Sneaky, kind of. Asking the same questions over and over. Trying to trip him up. The repetitious questions trying to confuse him about what he'd said.

Carrington watched him carefully. The truth never changes. It's a fact. If you tell the truth you don't have to remember what you said. But deception is sometimes difficult to remember. Especially the sequence of events and activities. What happened first? What next? What did you do? And then what happened? What did he do? Then what? Locking him into his story was important. And he was starting to tire. Carrington waited.

He should have gotten up and walked out right then and there but his curiosity about what they had on him kept him glued to his chair.

"So you guys got any of that DNA stuff they talk about all the time?"

Carrington couldn't believe him. "Huh, DNA?"

"Yeah, like C.S.I. on TV. I mean, the stuff to prove a rape, right?"

Carrington looked up, "Did I say she was raped?" The detective began to morph into a cat watching a humming bird.

He stared at the detective. He felt hot blood rush to his face and hoped it didn't show. Dammit. Didn't he say she was raped? No? But he had suggested it by reminding him of his prior rape convictions.

"No, I didn't say that, I just meant that . . . I've heard that they need DNA to prove a rape and I was just wondering. You need to have DNA to prove a murder? Like the O.J. case?"

Weak, thought Carrington. Weak explanation. The door was opening wider. He's going to slip an admission of guilt somewhere. Carrington couldn't believe this dipshit was still sitting here digging his own grave like he was getting paid overtime.

"What would you say if I told you we found your fingerprints inside that house?"

He blinked, "I'd say that's impossible." Carrington watched his Adam's apple contract.

"But you did admit that you were in the house when you brought the dog back, right?"

"Yeah, but . . ." He wondered where they had found his prints. Other than around the front door. He fought back a sudden urge to urinate.

Carrington leaned forward towards him and lowered his voice.

"Look, I don't know if you killed her. But, I mean . . . , like you could have. You had the opportunity. You were there." He paused for effect. "And you had the motive. Your prior record proves that."

He stared intently at Carrington wondering what they had.

"So maybe you just saw her one afternoon, and you said to yourself, I think I'll get me a little bit of that. But then something went wrong, she fought you or something, or it was the dog, or the telephone, and you just freaked out. Right?"

He sat up straight and leaned back in his chair to distance himself from the detective and the accusation, "No, I didn't kill nobody, man". He coughed into his hand again and wiped it on his pants leg. "You got the wrong guy."

Carrington leaned in closer and waited, using the silence to build the psychological pressure. He waited and mentally counted slowly to ten. The longer he waited, the stronger the urge would grow to fill the conversational space between the two of them. He waited for the silence to force a response. To fill the empty space. He looked directly at him while the silence in the box hung as heavy as a thick fog at the beach. Carrington looked into his watery eyes and waited. He was beginning to smell the fear that he knew was crawling up the back of his throat like battery acid.

"I don't know, man, this is gettin' pretty heavy", he wheezed. "I know I didn't kill nobody though." His heel started tapping on the floor.

Carrington sat motionless looking at him for another thirty seconds.

"Sit tight a minute, I'll be right back," he said abruptly.

He stood up leaving him hunched over the table in the box—before he could jump and run. Will was afraid he had pushed him too far. Then he turned back, holding the door open.

"Need to use the restroom, cup of coffee, soda or something?"

"No thanks, man. I'm good." Inside his guts had started to spasm.

Nick and Will stood outside the box watching him on the monitor. "Still haven't heard anything on the cell phone. Cindy is setting up the lineup for that witness across the street and Bobby is waiting for his former parole officer to call back. Nothing back from the lab yet on the latents. It'd sure be nice if we had the murder weapon. He looks like he's definitely starting to get the shakes but he just can't let it go. I expected him to lawyer up an hour ago, but this fool has got to find out what we have. It's killing him."

"Yeah, I can't believe he hasn't jumped up and run right out of here."

"What do you think about throwing the dog at him, see what he does with it", asked Nick.

"Yeah, I like that. Maybe he's not ready for me to really shove it down his throat. Let me see what I can do with the dog."

Carrington walked back into the box and placed a cup of coffee in front of him but he made no move for it.

"You said you found her dog in the street, is that right," he asked.

"Yeah, it was running loose and I caught it. Brought it back to her."

He hesitated, wondering where this was going. Have they searched his apartment? Did they find some dog hairs on him? Or blood? That damn dog. Kept barking. He'd had to shut it up. He also told himself he wasn't going to fall for that get the DNA off the coffee cup trick either. He didn't realize that he'd smeared DNA all over his shirt and pants every time he wiped his nose; and that he'd given it up the first time he'd been booked for rape years ago.

"What would you say if I told you that the dog never went in the front of the house? Because it was scared of the street? That it never left the back yard."

He hesitated, leaned back in his chair in a demonstration of confidence and folded his arms across his chest protectively.

"I'd say you're blowin' smoke", he replied, "I found it in the street. Who told you it never went out front?" Shit, he thought, I'm in trouble. That damn dog.

Carrington ignored his question. He knew it had started. Slowly peeling back the layers of lies and deception. The dog had been beaten to death, probably with the same weapon as the victim, thrown in the bathtub like a dirty towel.

"Would you be willing to take a polygraph test?" he suddenly asked.

"Oh man, I don't know. I'm so upset; you got me going here, you know, accusing me of killing someone. I'd probably set the thing on fire." He shook his head slowly. "I been to prison three times, man, I mean . . . I know how the world turns."

Carrington smiled. "Well, actually you're measured from a base point, and that would take into consideration your current condition. You know, how you're feeling. So whatever condition or state you're in right now, it accounts for that. You're evaluated against yourself. So it's all relative."

"I don't know, man. Those things scare me. I mean, who's to trust them things. I hear the results are pretty easy to manipulate. All those wires, and graphs and shit. I don't know. Anybody can say you're guilty and . . . ."

"Well, this gives you a chance to clear yourself. Once and for all," explained Carrington. "If you're innocent, like you say you are, you got nothing to be worried about. You pass the test, we're done with you, and you go home. That's it. It's that simple."

Carrington paused. "Now if you're guilty, I can understand how you'd be reluctant to take the test because it would show that. I mean, that you're guilty. So when you tell me you don't want to take it I can only think that you are guilty. Right? Know what I'm sayin'? Any innocent man would jump at the chance to prove his innocence."

He stared at the detective. Then looked down at the floor. "I don't think so, man. I just don't really trust those things. I know they don't use 'em in court. If they were legit, judges would let 'em in, right? I mean, they'd be OK. So if they can really tell you're lying, if they're really a hundred per cent reliable, how come they can't use them in court?"

Carrington felt a slow burn beginning to kindle under his collar. Smart ass. Read too many law books in the joint. But he was right. Polygraphs weren't admissible because they aren't considered flawless—too many variables creating too many subjective interpretations of truthfulness or deception. And many results were just simply inconclusive. No, the greatest benefit of the poly in the hands of a skilled operator is encouraging a confession by convincing the suspect that the witchcraft machine could spot a lie like a neon light in the desert at midnight.

Carrington went back at him.

"Look, man, I can understand how this happened. Something just went wrong. You didn't go in there planning to kill her. Something just . . . look. This crime was carried out by either a vicious remorseless killer—or someone who just freaked out. Someone who made a mistake. So, tell me you're not a vicious remorseless killer. You just made a mistake, right? Something just went wrong."

Watching the intensity ratchet up, Nick had waved over the other homicide detectives and they all stood in front of the monitor. Everyone held their breath as Will continued his well practiced rant. In his office the lieutenant stopped his reading and looked up at the monitor hanging on the wall in front of his desk.

Inside Carrington raised his voice, "Tell me you're not a vicious remorseless killer." He waited. "You're not a vicious killer, are you? Are you?"

"Tell me you're NOT a VICIOUS REMORSELESS KILLER."

He dropped his head down and slowly shook it from side to side. Carrington stared at his hands now clasped tightly in his lap. The pressure turned his fingernails white.

"Please, say it, man. Look at me." The detective reached out and grabbed his elbow, squeezing with increasing intensity, straining to make a connection. "C'mon, time to man up."

"You made a mistake. Something just went wrong, right?" He paused. "There had to be a reason for this, right?"

He ignored the detective's hand on his elbow.

"Tell me you're not a vicious remorseless killer."

Carrington's face blistered hot, and he felt a crescendo of anger building in him. He stood up, leaned on the desk with both arms and got in his face.

"C'mon man, TELL ME YOU'RE NOT A VICIOUS REMORSELESS KILLER!"

He backed away from him. "Tell me something went wrong. Something just went wrong. I know you didn't mean to kill her."

He looked up and then away from Carrington, towards the door, in a helpless effort to escape.

The detective's voice softened. "Just tell me it was a mistake."

He slumped in his chair and put his head in his hands. The tears started slowly, one at a time, and he struggled to hold them back. Gradually his body started to shake, and then he began to convulse uncontrollably. He coughed violently. Carrington leaned forward and carefully placed his hand on his shoulder, slowly massaging.

"It's over, my friend," he said. "The hard part is over. Let it out. Go ahead. Let it all out."

The detective waited patiently, saying nothing, knowing it was coming. The gush of emotion. The cleansing catharsis. An emotional orgasm—for both of them. And then it would be over. C'mon motherfucker, he thought, go ahead. Puke your evil guts out on my floor. Go ahead. You have my official permission. The quiet vibration of the overhead fluorescent lights suddenly began to irritate Carrington, as if small electrical wires attached to his skin were receiving a message. He hung on, but he desperately wanted it to be over. Gradually the sobbing subsided after several minutes. He nodded, looked up at Carrington through red rimmed eyes and cleared his throat.

"I want a lawyer."

Surprised, Carrington stared at him for a few seconds and then slammed his fist on the table. "Dammit! You bastard!" He stood up, leaned over the table and shoved his face at him. "You sorry mother-fucker." After what seemed to be forever, he walked out of the box and kicked the door shut.

Outside, he met Nick in the hallway who shook his head sympathetically.

"That's it, partner. It's over. Sorry, Will. His birdbrain finally fired up and saved his ass. If those Supreme Court bastards could witness what we just went through. How can a stone cold killer walk just by asking for a fuckin' lawyer? It's bullshit. Un—fucking—believable. No more questions and he walks right out of here. C'mon. I mean, it ain't like we're pulling out his fingernails or wiring his nuts to a car battery. Unbelievable. Totally, un—fucking—believable."

Will wandered down the hall to his cube shaking his head in anger and frustration.

Nick walked back to the box and opened the door. He motioned to him with a head nod.

Surprised, he stood up and slowly brushed by the detective as he walked out of the box and down the hall. When he reached the glass doors at front of the building he turned around, threw a bit of smirk at Nick, and walked out into a late afternoon sunset the color of a week-old bruise.

Nymphs, Terrestrials and Rainbows

THEY PARKED THE pickup truck under the trees in the clearing at the end of a deserted gravel road and unloaded their gear. The man and a boy about twelve. It didn't take them long. They had done this many times and they knew exactly what they needed. The fly rods were graphite nine footers, six weight, with light leaders and little drag on the reels. Both struggled into chest high waders, the boy with a set of neoprene hand-me-downs with a couple patches. He wore his lucky Snake River Fly Fishing baseball cap. Each pulled on a vest with all the equipment they'd need hanging on their chest. They also carried backpacks with all the basic survival essentials, and two quarts of water. The man slid a ten inch survival knife into the side of his pack and then withdrew a .45 caliber semi-automatic from a small canvas bag under the driver's seat. He checked the slide twice, pointed at the ground and pulled the trigger. Then he inserted a magazine, chambered a round and tucked it into the top of his pack. The boy watched without saying anything.

With slate gray eyes a little too small for his face and a pitted complexion the man had a hard look. He was tall, well over six feet, lean as a piece of beef jerky, with a kind of cowboy toughness about him. He didn't talk much and he radiated the threat of a silent man. Strangers weren't inclined to strike up a conversation with Ben Branson.

"Check your pepper spray, son," he said to the boy. "Just in case we run into a bear out there. And remember . . ."

"Yep, stay up wind and send the spray down to him. And if he charges ball up and cover my head." The boy grinned, knowing he'd remind him.

His father didn't smile. Bears could be serious trouble, but Ben worried a lot more about mountain lions. They didn't give you a chance. They were all about stalking, surprise, and attack. But they were going to work a large river together during the day and they'd pull out before dusk, the more dangerous time for the predators.

Ben watched carefully as the boy pulled out his red can of pepper spray. He licked a finger, held it up to check the wind direction, faced away from the wind and pulled the trigger. The short burst quickly dissipated in the gentle breeze. He flipped the safety on and slipped the can back into his pack.

Satisfied they had packed what they needed, Ben covered up the other rods and equipment and locked the camper shell. He handed an extra key to the boy who tucked it safely into the chest pouch of his waders.

"And don't mess with any rattlers, Robby. You got your snakebite kit?"

The boy nodded. "Yep."

They set out towards the river following a small path along the alders and cottonwoods occasionally running into marshy meadows that sucked at their boots and made the boy's lungs burn. He was fascinated by the river and he loved the sound and the smell of the rushing water. And the time with his father. He couldn't think of anything better than fly fishing with his father. They had been planning this trip for a month waiting for the spring storms to blow through the valley and the river to settle down. He'd had a hard time getting to sleep the night before and he was up at five thirty getting breakfast out of the way. By six he was packing his gear into the pickup while his father was just pouring his first cup of coffee.

They moved steadily upstream away from the widest stretch of the river where it picked up speed and eventually hit a falls of eighty feet which fell into a high walled canyon. A level four rapids followed the falls for a couple hundred yards before slowing and offering shore access. Above the falls, the river was wide, maybe forty, fifty yards for the first half mile, then began to narrow down as several separate fingers merged into the main flow. They made it a habit to fish well upstream from the falls. It was a gorgeous gift of nature and picture postcard beautiful. But deadly.

After an hour they stopped. Both were sweating heavily under their gear. Ben took off his worn Indiana Jones hat, wiped the sweat off the inside band and took a long drink of water. He wore the hat well, as if it had been a good friend for a long time, which it was. Robby took a couple swallows of water and then opened a power bar which he finished along the trail. The smell of the wild mint was overpowering and blended with the damp river air. They pushed on until they could hear the rushing of the water in the river at the narrows. Both increased their pace in anticipation of finding an access to the river. Several times they poked their way through the wild strawberry bushes and thick fescue grass to look over the river before returning to the path. Even though they'd fished here many times the river always looked new and raw to the boy. The third time they stopped Ben looked around and then nodded.

"OK, let's try this place. I'd start with a pheasant, or a hare's ear maybe, size sixteen or eighteen, they usually work for me. Don't forget a small lead shot to give you some depth. Now look at the river. Read the water. Where you gonna cast?"

Robby scanned the river gauging the depth and the current, noticing the boiling eddies, submerged rocks and back brush that could snare his flies. He pointed out a series of riffles at two o'clock with his rod. They formed a feeding trough for the fish in the river like the buffet line in his school cafeteria.

"Over there. Drift it over the steps of the riffles."

Ben nodded. "OK, good. I'll work upstream from you. Maybe thirty, forty yards. Don't wander off downstream. Don't wade in above your knees. And remember. You can't catch anything if your line isn't in the water. Good luck, son." With that he disappeared into the brush.

Robby opened the fly box clipped to his vest and studied the flies. Wet and dry surface flies, underwater nymphs, mayflies, woolly buggers, emergers, terrestrials, streamers. He must have had a hundred. A fly for every conceivable fish, water and weather condition. He fingered several of the flies, trying to decide. Rule number one, he knew, was that the fly had to be something of interest to the fish. Something it feeds on everyday. He considered fish lazier than cows, just lying on the bottom facing upstream, watching junk drift by, occasionally taking a nip at something that looked appetizing. And then the presentation. It had to be offered to them in a natural way, the way they usually see it. Shooting to the surface like an insect escaping its hatch, herky-jerky like an injured grasshopper, drifting lazily on the surface like an errant mosquito or a tired dragonfly. Each fly had its unique composition, color and characteristic movement—and purpose. That's where technique kicks in, Ben would say. And it's the reason Robby and his father could stand shoulder to shoulder casting in the same spot, using the same fly and Robby would come up empty. Don't worry about technique, his father always told him, you'll grow into it like learning to throw a curveball. One day you'll just realize you've got it.

Then there's the cast, the soul of fly fishing. Master the cast and you'll master fly fishing, Ben always said.

And sometimes a little misery helps. In some ways fly fishing is like duck hunting. The more miserable the weather, the more you suffer, the more luck you'll have. It's the old religious ethic of masochism. If it tastes good it's bad for you, and if it feels good you probably shouldn't be doing it. You can catch trout on a warm sunny day, but you'll probably catch more in a cold blinding rainstorm. Regardless, Ben always said, the Church of the Rainbow Trout will always remain a spiritual experience that can turn you into a poet or a philosopher.

Robby finally decided on a size sixteen beaded pheasant and quickly tied it to the tippet. He attached the tippet to four pound line, graduated to six, and then to the actual weight forward fly line on the reel. He tested each knot with his teeth before trimming it.

He took his time, knowing the knots were important, but also enjoying the anticipation of the fishing itself. Much of his satisfaction came from planning and anticipating the actual time on the river. The sight, the sound and the smell of the rushing water triggered all his senses and sometimes made him lightheaded. He could spend an entire day on the river by himself totally engrossed in a search for the big one, which he usually tossed back to grow up and get smarter. He had been well taught by his father to catch and release and he'd outgrown the need to bring a rainbow home to show off to his mother years ago.

He snaked out about fifteen feet of line and began casting upstream from the riffles. Elbow tight to his side using his wrist like he'd been taught, gradually increasing the length of the line, finally laying the fly gently down on the surface above the roiling water. Robby reminded himself to slow down his back cast to avoid hooking the fly on his hat or tangling the line. What's the hurry, his father always asked. He rapidly mended the line keeping it taut, watching the white strike indicator as it slowly drifted down river.

Any hesitation or dip down and he'd tip up to set the hook. He repeated his cast several times with no response and then suddenly had a strike.

Just a nudge, something a novice probably wouldn't have noticed, but enough to tell Robby a fish was lying there, looking things over. He'd come up and tongued the fly out of curiosity, but rejected it or lost interest. Technique, Robby reminded himself. Technique. He crouched forward to reduce his profile, shook the water from his line with two more casts and gently laid the fly back on the water. He knew he'd probably only get one more chance before this one got smart. He mended carefully, watching the indicator float downstream. When it suddenly hesitated, he ripped up the rod tip and felt the fish tug on the end. It immediately ran to the middle of the river and Robby laughed out loud as the line unwinding from the reel started to sing. When it stopped he quickly wound up the slack.

Five minutes later he pulled the exhausted rainbow up in front of him in three feet of water along the bank. A fifteen incher, brilliantly multi-colored, mouth open in fatigue, gills moving slowly. He reached around his back, and pulled out his net. As he brought it in front of him the fish noticed and dug down into the river to avoid capture. He kept the tension on the line and waited patiently. Another couple minutes and he gently towed it over to the bank. He slowly slid the net under the fish, lifting the rainbow up to the surface of the water. It smacked its tail in frustration, rolling over in the net, refusing to give up. Robby grinned admiring its fight. Tucking his rod under his arm, he held the fish firmly while he slipped the fly out of its mouth. Still in the net, he lowered the fish back into the water, petted its head twice, and set it free. It disappeared in a silver flash. He looked up stream in the direction of his father, but he was out of sight. Grinning to himself, he wound up his fly line and moved on further up the river.

By noon Robby had caught a half dozen fifteen to twenty inch rainbows. His success allowed him to slow down a bit and enjoy the moment, realizing that he no longer had anything to prove. To himself. Or to his father. No, he was definitely good at this. He looked around at the woods and the river, filled his lungs with the fragrant river air, and reminded himself that he was one lucky dude.

When the water became shallower, he switched to a size 18 beige caddis and a smaller shot and caught two more. Smaller, but gorgeous, spunky fish. One stood up and walked away on its tail showing off as if its girlfriend was watching. Robby admired its spirited fight. An hour later he wound up his line and headed upstream to check on his father. Along the way he stopped to relieve himself, laughing as he watered a waving aspen. There was something primitive and a bit exciting about pissing in the woods. A demonstration of freedom, independence, a controlled recklessness—and a rite of passage. An entry into a man's world—his father's world.

When he found his father they both laughingly exaggerated the number and size of the rainbows they had caught. Ben even claimed to have hooked a monster brown trout until it broke the line with a desperate run upstream to hide under a submerged tree branch. Robby unwrapped the ham and cheese sandwiches his mother had prepared the night before along with a leftover slice of apple pie which had melted in his pack. He had bought a bottle of cherry coke at the bait shop that always gave him a stomach ache but which he refused to admit to his father. Ben drank peach tea. He was proud of his son's success and often thought it was one of the best gifts he had given him. Robby had finally mastered the art of patience which was so much a part of fly fishing. Some days he had even been more successful than his father, something they both enjoyed. Beginners luck, Ben always said. But inwardly he was proud of his son's developing skills.

Eventually they stood up and packed up their gear. They would have stayed longer but the black ants had finally arrived begging to share their lunch. It reminded Ben of that time back in Vietnam when a pack of red ants had emptied his tank quicker than an RPG. Robby had heard the story a dozen times but they still laughed together while he stashed their trash in his pack like his father had taught him. He had also become a good student of ecology and responsible environmentalism over the years.

They wandered further upstream hitting the various forks coming into the main river but with dwindling success as the day wore on. The water became slower and shallower as they continued north and things slowed down. Both changed flies often trying to match the intensity of the sun, the changing colors and characteristics of the river but gradually their luck ran out. As the sun slipped down behind the mountain angry storm clouds blew in threatening rain. The wind picked up and rippled the surface of the water forcing the fish to hunker down and stop eating. By late afternoon a chill had crawled into their sweaty clothes and they decided to move back down the river towards the rapids and the truck.

An hour later they finally wrapped up their gear and found their way back to the path. A stiff breeze had arrived with the storm clouds and it rustled in the cottonwoods like a stranger following them. Several times Robby stopped to listen, working to convince himself that they were alone. Forty minutes of pushing down the trail and they were almost to the clearing when they heard the sound of glass breaking. They stopped and looked at each other. Ben put his finger to his lips and waved them off the trail. They moved slowly and quietly through the cottonwoods towards the truck trying to avoid stepping on broken branches and making any noise. At the edge of the clearing they stopped and watched a man pulling gear out of the smashed rear window of their pickup. He dragged two of the fishing rods down to the edge of the river and stashed them in a sixteen foot aluminum boat. Turning around he hurried back to the truck and began rooting around in the rear seat storage compartment. They watched as he opened a beer from the cooler, pounded half down and crawled back into the bed of the truck. He threw out a sleeping bag and a tackle box and was busy checking the pockets of a rain jacket when Ben crept up behind him.

"What the hell are you doing in my truck, you sonafabitch?" Ben yelled.

The man turned around and looked directly into the barrel of Ben's .45 automatic.

"What the . . ." his voice stopped as Ben grabbed his arm and pulled him out of the bed of the pickup. He never had a chance. He landed on his face and Ben pounced on him like a junkyard dog. He stuck the .45 into his right ear.

"Get your pepper spray, Robby", he yelled.

The boy dropped his pack and quickly found the canister. He handed it to his father who muscled the man onto his side. Ben took the can from Robby and flipped the safety off. Then he painted his face with the pepper spray blinding him.

Ben straddled the man who was much smaller and shoved his face into the ground. He slid the .45 into the pouch of his waders and handed the pepper spray back to Robby.

"Give me your duct tape."

Robby dug back into his pack and handed the roll to his father who pinned the man's arms behind his back and quickly wrapped the wrists with the duct tape. It hardly seemed necessary as the man lay groaning on the ground, sightless, and completely vulnerable.

"Stealing our gear, eh?"

The man gagged on the pepper spray, and moaned. His eyes had snapped shut and he couldn't seem to talk. He was short and scrawny, with long greasy hair hanging over his ears. He wore dirty jeans, old cowboy boots, and a sweaty green T-shirt. He had a week's beard, tattoos on both arms and looked like he'd just walked out of the county jail. A human weasel.

He had trouble talking.

"I'm burning up, man," he wheezed. "Look, I was jus' checking this stuff out, I wasn't gonna . . ."

Ben interrupted him. "You broke into our truck and you were stealing our gear."

He rolled him over into a seating position on the ground. "Is that your boat over there?"

"Yeah, look man. I'm dying; my face is on fuckin' fire." His eyes remained glued shut and tears rolled down his cheeks. Snot poured out of his nose. His face was red and puffy.

Ben looked down at him with disgust. "Get up."

He helped him up and they stumbled down to the riverbank. When they reached the water Ben dragged him into the river, shoved him down and held his head underwater.

Robby's eyes widened and he yelled. "Dad!"

After thirty seconds or so Ben pulled him out of the water and dragged him back onto the shore. The man was gasping and vomiting on the riverbank. The boy stood back watching, his stomach roiling. He couldn't believe what he was seeing.

"That put the fire out for ya?" Ben snarled at the man. "What's your name, shitbird?"

The man continued choking. Ben slapped the back of his head. Twice. Hard. He looked up, eyes still shut.

"Eddie. Eddie Montague."

"OK, Eddie, let's check out your boat. See what you been stealin'."

He pushed Eddie over to the boat, which was pulled up on the bank. Robby trailed behind, spellbound. A small anchor was thrown about fifteen feet ahead of the boat even though the water only lapped at the edge of the river. A beat up 7.5 horsepower Mercury outboard motor on the transom was pulled forward with the prop sticking out of the water. Robby's birthday fly rod and two others were lying on the floor of the boat along with a set of weather beaten oars. He'd also thrown in an extra pair of Ben's hip boots, their small Honda generator and a six pack of beer.

"Where'd you come from?" Ben asked.

"'Across the river, man, my truck's over there. I was doing a little trolling when my motor gave out. Had to row over to the side here."

"Your motor died on you while you were trolling?"

"Yeah, can't afford a new one though," he hacked and gagged and tried to open his eyes.

"Where's your fishing rod? You said you were trolling."

"I, ah, . . . look . . ."

"You lying sack of shit. You're nothin' but a goddam thief."

Ben looked out over the river and then at Robby. "What do you think we ought to do with this guy, son?"

The man tried to look at Ben but he couldn't keep his eyes open.

"Look man, I jus' made a mistake. Things been tough lately, ya know? How about we just forget about this whole thing and I get the hell out of here? You got your stuff back."

"What do you think, Robby?" Ben asked the boy again.

"I don't know dad, we did get everything back." He was fighting back tears. "Maybe we should just call the cops." He swallowed rapidly trying to push down the acid climbing up the back of his throat.

"Got no cell phone service out here, son. No cops, no park rangers. We got to handle this ourselves with a little frontier justice. How about we just send Eddie back across the river? He can paddle his way over to the other side."

Eddie blinked rapidly and tried to look at Ben. "Hey man, I told you that motor gave out. I don't know if I can row all the way across. And that rapids is movin' pretty fast. If I don't make it I could go over the falls."

"Well, you got about a hundred yards to find out, asshole. Son, pull all our gear out of there and throw that anchor back in the boat."

The boy did as he was instructed. Eddie watched him carefully, blinking nonstop, with runny, bloodshot eyes. His wrists were still taped behind his back.

"You can't do this to me, man. C'mon", he pleaded.

Watching him carefully over his shoulder, Ben walked over to his pack and pulled out his survival knife. Eddie looked at the huge knife fearfully as he approached.

Ben stood over Eddie holding the knife out in his right hand as if he were offering to show him something. Suddenly he dropped down with a knee in the middle of his chest forcing a grunt. He stuck the point of the blade in the side of his throat.

"I oughta cut your goddam throat", he snarled. Eddie tried to roll away but was pinned by the knee in his chest. As he struggled Ben continued to push the knifepoint. Robby inched forward in disbelief and noticed a red trickle of blood starting to run down the side of Eddie's neck. He fought back the urge to throw up.

After what seemed to be an hour to Robbie, Ben stood up and wrestled Eddie to his feet. He pushed him back down to the river and shoved his head under the water again. Coughing and choking he finally jerked him up and cut off the duct tape around his wrists. Robbie watched silently cowering at the back of the pickup.

"Now get in that boat, asshole, and get the hell outa here", he growled.

Eddie hesitated a bit which gave Ben a reason to push him into the boat. He stumbled and then fell clumsily landing on his left shoulder. He sat up and rubbed his shoulder.

Ben leaned into the boat and grabbed both the oars.

"Hey, whaddya doin', man, you can't take my oars."

Ben laughed. "That's exactly what I'm doing. You can paddle with your hands."

Ben shoved the boat with Eddie Montague out into the river. He watched him for a couple minutes and then waded into the water and threw one of the oars in the direction of the boat. It planed briefly, stopped and then drifted just out of reach of the boat. Ben was surprised Eddie didn't throw the anchor overboard to try to slow the boat. He turned to Robby who had wandered down closer to the river.

"Life's about choices, son. He can stay in that boat and paddle himself, or jump out and get that oar and swim back to the boat. Or he can swim to shore. What do you think he ought to do?"

Robby shook his head without answering. He couldn't take his eyes off Eddie in the boat.

Eddie stood up in the boat and screamed. "I ain't a good swimmer, man, you can't do this to me."

He looked fearfully at the falls downriver. And then back at the oar floating ten yards away. He kneeled down and started paddling on one side of the boat. Then the other side to straighten it out. Looking down river, he stood up and ran to the back of the boat. He pushed the motor into the water, primed it, and started pulling on the starter. It coughed but failed. He gave it several more pulls and then knelt down again, groaning in anger and frustration, and started paddling. He stood up again but he'd lost sight of the oar as it floated by him. He looked back at the bank of the river in desperation.

The man and the boy stood on the bank watching him.

Robby, mesmerized, suddenly looked up at his father. "Dad, he may not make it."

Ben stood impassively watching the boat drift slowly downstream.

They watched Eddie hanging over the side of the boat paddling with his hands and arms. It had drifted almost into the middle of the river and the current began pulling at it. He increased his paddling and tried to aim for the bank but the boat continued to move downstream. He stood up in the middle of the boat, balanced precariously, and screamed something unintelligible at them.

Robby looked up at his father, but neither said anything.

The boat picked up speed and Eddie began paddling furiously. He desperately moved from one side to the other but it seemed to make no difference. He stood up again as if trying to decide whether to jump and swim for it. But then he knelt down and hung off the side of the boat looking for a rock or something poking out of the water to grab a hold of.

They watched it approach the mouth of the falls, bumping a rock hidden just under the surface which twisted the boat sideways momentarily. Then it straightened out again, the front bow dug down and the rear suddenly popped up for a second throwing the man up and out of the boat. Then they both disappeared over the rapids.

Robby looked up at his father who stared straight ahead. Neither said anything. They stood still for several minutes before Ben picked up the second oar and threw it far out into the river. Then he turned around and walked back to the truck. Robby stared hard at the river half expecting Eddie to reappear. After several minutes he turned around and followed after his father.

When he reached the pickup, Ben turned to his son. He put his hand roughly on his shoulder and looked him in the eye. He spoke ominously, in a tone of voice Robby had never heard before.

"Son, we must never speak of this again. Do you understand?"

The boy swallowed the lump in his throat and nodded. He turned away so his father wouldn't see the tears welling up in his eyes.

A half mile upstream on a bluff overlooking the river ornithologist Bryson Jennings had been watching a condor nest across the river. He was hoping for a glimpse of the proud parents bringing food to the noisy chick nestled high in the trees. He was well concealed in a thicket of bushes at the edge of the bluff and had trained himself to remain still for long periods of time. His attention had been drawn to the human activity downstream when he'd noticed the movement of the two men and a boy on the shore of the river. There was an obvious dispute of some kind, that was apparent even at a distance. He had trained his Bushnell PowerView binoculars on the trio and observed the scene play out. He watched with horror as the man in the boat drifted down the river and went over the falls. Jennings was well familiar with the area and knew the fate that awaited the man. Even if he survived the falls, and he probably wouldn't, the rapids lay in wait for him like a hungry beast. When the man and the boy disappeared from the riverbank he quickly made his way back to his mud splattered Honda Element parked at the trailhead. His intention was to drive down the mountain and wait for his cell phone coverage to click on, but just as he began to pull out a light green pickup truck drove into the parking area.

The U.S. Park ranger hopped out of the pickup, adjusted his gun belt and walked towards the restrooms. Jennings pulled alongside him, stopped, and rolled down his window.

"Excuse me, sir, got a minute?"

7th Street Blue Line

T HEY STOOD WAITING patiently at the Grand Street bus stop. She was early thirties, Hispanic, pushing a baby stroller with an infant tucked securely inside. A small girl about two, wearing a yellow hooded ski jacket, clung to one of the handlebars of the stroller. The boy stood next to his mother wearing a Scooby-Doo backpack that was about as big as the boy. He bent forward and his arms hung down in front of him to balance the pack. There were several others waiting for the bus but none of them spoke to each other.

A few minutes later the 7th Street Blue Line pulled over to the curb and the door creaked open for the waiting riders who bunched up at the bottom of the steps. The driver leaned forward on the steering wheel, staring straight ahead and paid no attention to those getting on. The boy held back and looked up at his mother. He was nine years old but somewhat skinny and looked a couple years younger. She bent over and gave him a hug, whispered a few words to him, and gently nudged him towards the bus. She had noticed that he had begun acting a little clingy waiting for the bus lately, and that he had seemed to be losing interest in school. And he'd been spending more time with his video games in the apartment than playing with the other kids in the neighborhood. She was worried about him and probed gently but he was unresponsive and became even more withdrawn. His father could help, maybe, but he wasn't going to be released for three more months.

The boy finally moved to the door and climbed the steps looking over his shoulder at his mother. He walked down the aisle and took a seat along side the window like his mother insisted so he could wave goodbye to her. She smiled outside and waved at him as the bus gradually wheezed away from the curb.

As it started moving the boy looked around at the other passengers. They all stared straight ahead, sitting silently as if in a self contained bubble, oblivious to the others. He wondered if there were bus rules prohibiting talking to others. He watched anxiously as people got on one by one at each stop. He didn't see the man but he knew it was three more stops anyway. He fidgeted with the heavy back pack sitting on his lap. The familiar fumes from the bus always made him nauseous. If his ride had been ten minutes longer he was sure he'd throw up his breakfast burrito.

San Pedro. Washington. The boy tensed up more with each stop.

Finally, Vernon. He looked out the window but he didn't see him. Maybe he wouldn't get on today, the boy prayed. He watched several riders get on. An elderly black couple, a woman in a nurse's uniform, a homeless guy mumbling and wearing two jackets, and then . . . . the man. He was the last to get on. Dressed like always. Green Sears work pants, blue jean jacket and work shoes with white paint on the toes. Always those work shoes. And the dirty Dodgers baseball hat.

The man shuffled down the aisle seemingly paying no attention to anyone, searching for an open seat. Unable to find a seat next to someone else, the boy had moved over to the aisle hoping the man wouldn't push his way into the empty window seat. But then, as the man reached the boy, he stopped, hesitated, and then without looking at him, slid into the window seat. The boy was immediately stung by the smell of stale cigarettes and coffee. And the man smell. He recoiled unconsciously and hugged his backpack. The man stared straight ahead holding an Albertson's supermarket brown paper bag on his lap. Probably his lunch. The boy's breathing became more rapid as his anxiety increased. He looked around at the other riders. None paid any attention to him.

Minutes passed. Then the man placed his hand on the boy's right leg. The boy sucked in a breath feeling like he had been stabbed in the chest. He stared down at the hand for a moment. Brown, large veins, dirty fingernails. He looked around again. The couple across the aisle leaned on each other and appeared to be dozing, one of the students wearing iPod earplugs was nodding along with the music with his eyes closed, and the homeless man had stretched out across two seats and seemed to be sleeping. The boy stole a furtive glance at the man who continued to stare straight ahead. He looked down at the paint stained work shoes. A wave of helplessness washed over the boy and he shivered with anticipation.

After a few more minutes, the man's hand slid down into the boy's crotch. He recoiled and looked around. His face felt hot and he fought back tears. As the man started to stroke the boy he struggled to catch his breath. He felt like he was drowning. He swallowed fast choking back the bile rising in his throat. How many more stops? And then, suddenly, the man stood up and brushed past the boy. He waited nonchalantly at the rear door, and at the next stop he stepped down off the bus and stood on the corner waiting for the light to change. The light changed and the man walked off.

The boy wiped the tears from his eyes and settled back into his seat like the others who were still staring straight ahead. The smell of the man burned his eyes. Two stops later the boy got off the bus at Firestone. He adjusted his backpack, crossed with the light and fell in with the crowd of students heading towards the middle school.

211 P.C.

OFFICERS SERGIO GONZALEZ and Charles Hollingsworth had been pushing 3-Zebra-12 for the last nine months and had become living legends. As a Zebra patrol unit they weren't assigned the routine neighborhood disputes, bar fights, and wife beater calls, but instead handled the hot shots in their sector. Shots fired, robbery in progress, vehicle pursuit, gang activity, officer needs assistance. It was high speed liquid adrenalin and they prided themselves on often working straight through a ten hour shift without a Code 7 break for a meal. They were the hot shit stars of the station and they drove their senior patrol sergeant, Ben Fitzgerald, fucking nuts.

Fitzgerald was a classic worrier who went through life with his foot on the brake, constantly waiting for The Bad Thing to happen. A life long OCD'er, he showered three times a day, washed his hands every twenty minutes, refused to shake hands with anyone, and carried two bottles of hand sanitizer. Everything was gloom and doom, and infectious. He wouldn't fly on an airplane unless he could book an exit seat over the wing, and he Googled the safety record of the aircraft model before making a reservation. After 9-11 he carried a rope ladder in a gym bag when he visited Las Vegas and refused to accept a hotel room above the 3rd floor. A month after the Northridge earthquake he had turned his garage into a completely functional command post stocked with enough water for his home owners association for a month, a pallet of ready-to-eat military rations, a Cabela's sports Porta-Potty and reams of toilet paper which he planned to sell to his neighbors after the first week. He had purchased a dozen rifles and collected cases of ammo designed to hold off the hordes of hungry homeless hunting for food once the revolution started. He tested his ham radio system weekly by calling Thailand or Romania or finding someone in Bumfucke, Egypt who would answer. He kept enough Cipro in his refrigerator for the whole family if the terrorists started the attack with anthrax. Potential intermittent explosive disorder (IED) with skyrocketing blood pressure and stuttering was his default setting. Yes, Ben Fitzgerald was a worrying man.

And now, these two ticking bombs, referred to as Gasoline and Matches by the other officers, had been assigned to him. Both had been involved in several shooting incidents which made the others around them a little uneasy. People looked at them a little sideways since they'd pulled the trigger a few times. They didn't want to ride with them either. And as if the number of use of force complaints against the 3-Zebra-12 team wasn't enough to land both of them on the department Watch List of overly aggressive officers, Gonzalez and Hollingsworth also led the station in sexual harassment complaints. Between the two of them they had tried out every attractive female in the Records Department resulting in an epidemic of the woman scorned syndrome. At the mere mention of Gonzalez or Hollingsworth, Fitzgerald would launch into a series of nervous tics like a third base coach signaling for a hit and run. Compared to the carnivorous, heavily inked, and buffed up gym rats he was responsible for, Fitzgerald was about as muscular as a ball point pen. He was a strict vegetarian who usually ate something resembling crushed dandelions and tree bark which he brought to work each day in a small plastic baggie.

They were also the practical jokers in the station and both had been involved in infamous capers in the department. Hollingsworth had won the underground department contest challenging the officers to drive a marked black and white patrol vehicle as far away from the city limits as possible during an eight hour shift. The winner for over a year had been a run to Las Vegas.

But Hollingsworth had a better plan. His brother had been stationed at an Air Force base east of the city and assigned to a C-141 cargo aircraft wing. Hollingsworth had driven his unit out to the air base and into the C-141 with his brother flying a check ride to St. Louis, Missouri. And when he touched down at Scott AFB Hollingsworth roared the black and white out of the C-141 and sped to the famous arch where his brother photographed him leaning against it with the "Welcome to St. Louis" sign in the background. He had taken off his nametag, of course, and wore a Hulk Hogan mask so none of the brass could identify him. But everyone knew. Mostly because Hollingsworth bragged that he had bought a new Harley with the winnings he collected.

Gonzalez had been involved in the infamous hotel duck shooting in Sacramento three years ago at the annual conference of the state narcotics officers. After an afternoon of bullshit war stories and hammering down shots of tequila with his dope buddies in the hotel bar, they were surprised to witness the return of the ducks like the swallows to Capistrano. Each afternoon, when the sun went down, a dozen white ducks from the outside pond would make their way back through a small canal into the larger pool in the middle of the hotel to typically entertain the visiting conventioneers. Watching the ducks proudly paddle in one after another, one of the cops slyly mentioned that he hadn't been to a shooting arcade for years. Within seconds, they had all pulled their guns and began to pick off the ducks as they swam into the lobby. After four hits, which even amazed them, they fled the hotel like they'd just pulled off an armored car heist.

By the time the local cops arrived, the only description witnesses could offer was a bunch of drunken cops from out of town. The narcotics association pledged complete cooperation with the local police department of course, but no one was ever identified. Every one of the officers found in the hotel claimed to be in the restroom when it happened and insisted they had witnessed nothing. And in a typical display of uncooperativeness the police union stood up in front of polygraphs suggested for the attendees so eventually they all skated and no one was disciplined.

When he returned from the conference, Gonzalez, of course, bragged about personally bagging two of the ducks himself, but he was never officially charged. He became a hero within the association and each year at the annual conference the narcotics officer who had made the largest undercover dope bust was awarded a coveted white plastic duck named Sergio.

Every thing they did seemed to result in another internal investigation. Everything they touched turned radioactive. Trying to counsel them was like talking to mud. Fitzgerald had long ago lost any hope of promotion or transfer and was now just praying that he could hang on long enough to retire and keep his pension. He had begged for a transfer, even going to the emasculating training and plans division, but he didn't have enough wood on the captain to make it happen. He went to work each day with the trepidation of a man on his way to his first bungee jump and he was absolutely convinced that someday one of these street rat crazies was going to kill him or his career for good.

Three months ago the officers in 3-Zebra-12 had been involved in the pursuit of a carjacked SUV which terminated in a collision with a pickup. The driver of the pickup, apparently unhurt but definitely pissed, jerked the suspect out of the SUV and tore into him like a junkyard dog. Hollingsworth and Gonzalez arrived seconds later and stood critiquing the battle from the sidelines without making an effort to separate the two combatants.

After a couple minutes when they figured it had gone on long enough, Gonzales yelled, "OK dude, that's it. Round one is over."

But when both refused to stop, a witness later stepped forward and reported that she had overheard Gonzalez say, "OK, partner, go on and light up this motherfucker."

And light him up he did. With 50,000 volts from his trusty Taser, Hollingsworth had missed the suspect and instead fired both barbs into the back of the innocent truck driver making him dance the happy chicken.

Both officers were appropriately apologetic, but when the truck driver regained his senses and remembered his name he threatened to end Hollingsworth's police career. And when the use of force report was written, and the actions of the officers at the termination of the pursuit were reviewed, both Hollingsworth and Gonzales again became the subject of another internal affairs investigation. Their third since they had transferred into the station and been assigned to Sgt. Fitzgerald. Normally they would have been placed in an administrative assignment pending the outcome of the investigation, but due to a recent rash of workers comp injuries the station was short of available patrol officers. As a result the station commander had decided to allow them to remain in patrol while the investigation was being conducted. They also consistently led the station in arrest stats which made the patrol lieutenant look like he knew what he was doing.

There was just no relief or respite for Ben Fitzgerald.

When the "two-eleven" alarm call came out, Fitzgerald was sitting at his desk in the station reviewing the monthly racial profiling patrol reports. He glanced up when the hallway speaker came alive with the hot shot call and then shook his head when the two-eleven was assigned to Hollingsworth and Gonzalez. Section 211 of the Penal Code referred to the crime of robbery, and in the interest of brevity the police officers and dispatchers used the numbers of the penal code to describe the various calls. It had become the coded language of the police cult.

"3-Zebra-12, 3-Zebra-12, two eleven alarm, at the Arco mini-mart, 46th and Central."

Sitting under a dirty umbrella leaning over a rusted picnic table outside Mama's Hometown Cooking a half mile away, Hollingsworth and Gonzalez flinched when they heard the radio transmission. Their adrenalin started to pump like a hot shot of methamphetamine into a main vein. Leaving their barbecued pulled pork sandwiches steaming on the table, they ran to the black and white parked at the curb.

A minute later the dispatcher upgraded the call, "3-Zebra-12, and additional available units, two eleven in progress, at the Arco mini-mart, 46th and Central, multiple suspects, inside the mini-mart."

Hollingsworth and Gonzales looked at each other and grinned. They lived for this shit.

Three minutes later 3-Z-12 pulled off 46th street and swung into the western side of the Arco Mini mart. Gonzales hid the black and white alongside an empty pickup parked around the corner from the pumps. Nothing looked unusual.

Hollingsworth unlocked the Remington 870 shotgun between them and slipped it from the cradle. He chambered a round, inserted a fifth into the magazine and pushed the safety off. Gonzales pulled the 9mm Beretta from his holster and rested it along side his leg. Seconds later two black guys ran out of the front door towards a black Cadillac Escalade parked alongside the pumps. One had what appeared to be a short rifle.

"Well, looky there", muttered Hollingsworth. "We got us a couple of the brothers pullin' a big time stick-up job."

Gonzales edged the black and white out from behind the pickup and then tromped on it bringing the unit to within ten yards and perpendicular to the Escalade. Hollingsworth jumped out with the shotgun, assumed a defensive position behind the door, and yelled.

"Hold it right there, asshole. Show me your fuckin' hands!"

Gonzales took a similar position on the driver's side of the black and white.

"Get going, niggar, drive this mutha-fucka right at 'em", snarled the passenger to the driver of the Escalade.

The Escalade started moving slowly.

"Stop or I'll blow your fucking head off", yelled Hollingsworth, but the Escalade continued on.

Suddenly it took a vicious turn directly at the officers crouched on either side of their unit and gunfire from the passenger blew out the windshield of the black and white.

Both officers opened up simultaneously. Hollingsworth with the shotgun and Gonzalez with his Beretta. Hollingsworth pumped five rounds of buckshot from his shotgun into the windshield of the Escalade and watched it splinter and then explode. Gonzalez continued to fire his Beretta as the Escalade kept moving at them. It slowed down and gradually rolled to a stop a few feet in front of them. Both officers waited, expecting the occupants to barrel out and run but the shooting from inside the Escalade had stopped. Gonzales took the opportunity to slap a new magazine into his Beretta. Hollingsworth dropped his empty shotgun on the seat, drew his Beretta and cautiously approached the Escalade, looking inside. The driver was slumped over the wheel, and the passenger, bleeding from an apparent chest wound, looked at him helplessly. Suddenly a third suspect popped up in the rear seat, throwing his hands up in the air, arms shaking. Hollingsworth instinctively jerked back and fired several times into the back seat. The suspect took two rounds in the chest and one in the side of the neck which almost blew him over the back of the seat. Then he flopped forward and slipped to the floor, gasping.

Hollingsworth danced around the Escalade pointing his gun at each of the three robbers, threatening them individually. "Don't move asshole, I'll send you to Jesus."

Gonzalez had followed him around the vehicle, pulled out the passenger and handcuffed him. The driver looked dead, hanging over the steering wheel. A large red hole just to the side of his left eye gushed bright red blood. Hollingsworth kept his gun pointed at the suspect in the rear seat who was glassy eyed and having trouble breathing. His neck was covered in blood.

When Gonzalez had finished with the passenger and the driver, Hollingsworth pulled the third suspect out of the back seat, hooked him up and laid him face down along side the rear tire of the Escalade. He was small but dead weight.

He was also a kid. Maybe fifteen or sixteen. He looked up at Hollingsworth, and slurred, "Where'd I get hit?"

"You took a couple rounds, kid", coughed Hollingsworth, "Where'd you hide the gun?"

He said nothing, his eyes rolling.

"What's your name?"

"Poo . . . kie".

"Oh yeah, Pookie? Well, you and your homies did a pretty dumb ass thing today. And you got yourself shot to shit for it. Ya fucked up, dude."

It didn't look like Pookie was going to make it either. His eyes were beginning to take on that faded gray look and he lay motionless on the ground, breathing shallowly.

Gonzalez came around the corner of the Escalade looking a little bug eyed. "You OK?"

Hollingsworth looked up, "Yeah. You find the gun?"

"Yeah, it was laying on the floor on the passenger side," answered Gonzalez. "Ruger Mini 14 with the stock cut down."

"Jesus. That's some serious shit."

"Yeah. What about the kid," asked Gonzalez, "He have a piece?"

"Didn't find one", answered Hollingsworth. "I did see him make a furtive movement though. I thought he was goin' for one."

"Well, shit, that's all you need then", Gonzalez said slowly reciting from the training manual on the use of deadly force. "You faced an immediate threat to your life, right? And you were justified in using deadly force to prevent death or great bodily injury to yourself and others around you. All you need to see is that furtive movement. You thought he was goin' for a gun, right?"

"Yeah . . . yeah, that's how it was, partner," Hollingsworth smiled, nodding his head.

"OK, I'll notify dispatch", responded Gonzalez. "We're 10-15 with three suspects, all down; we've had an OIS, and request a rescue ambulance and a supervisor. And a second RA."

Gonzales returned to the black and white unit and sat down in the driver's seat. He hesitated for a moment, took a several deep breaths to slow and regulate his breathing, and then picked up the radio mike.

Hollingsworth looked around the scene and then walked back to the patrol unit. He opened the trunk and took out a roll of yellow crime scene tape and a pair of black leather gloves from underneath the spare. Then he walked over to the Escalade and leaned into the rear seat compartment. He put on one of the gloves and opened the other. A small gray two inch revolver slid out of the glove. He put on the other glove and then carefully tucked the gun between the rear seat and the armrest for the CSI guys to find. He backed out and began stringing the "Crime Scene, Do Not Cross" tape around the shooting scene.

Four minutes later the first of several additional units skidded into the driveway of the mini-mart. Code three, lights and siren. Hollingsworth greeted them with a nod to the suspects proned out on the ground.

"Me and Gonzalez, here, just taking care of business, guys. Just taking care of business. We took our limit and bagged three. Two are keepers. We'll have to throw the kid back in." Hollingsworth laughed nervously and grinned at the other cops who didn't.

Sgt. Fitzgerald drove into the mini-mart knowing that he was looking at the end of his career. Shots fired. Excessive force. Wrongful death. He could see the lawsuits coming. As their superior officer he'd be named as a principal in the lawsuit just like Hollingsworth and Gonzalez and everyone else in sight. The patrol supervisor, the police chief, the mayor, everyone in the chain of command. And probably the councilman who represented this district. Five years from now he'd be sitting in a federal courtroom sweating his ass off trying to explain what these two fuck-ups had just done.

Gonzalez grinned at him as he walked up. "Oh, oh, you caught us workin', sarg."

Fitzgerald didn't laugh. Although he had discovered a long time ago that he didn't care every time someone died, this thing had all the germs of a full blown cluster fuck.

"We think they're Grape Street Crips, boss. Tryin' ta pick up a little spending money for the weekend."

The sergeant first listened to a brief explanation of what had occurred from Gonzalez and then separately from Hollingsworth. Fortunately neither had asked for a union rep. And for the most part their response and actions taken seemed to be within department guidelines and policy. At least for now. He looked around and took in the rest of the scene.

Air 12 hovered at four hundred feet over the Arco station drowning out communication on the ground as usual. Paramedics from a second RA had arrived and joined the others treating the injured suspects. None of them looked like they'd make it but Fitzgerald knew crooks had an amazing way of beating the odds. Additional uniformed officers were sealing the shooting scene for the CSI people and a pack of coatless cops wearing their guns in the open like genitals on short haired street dogs milled around the gas pumps getting organized. Bystanders had begun to cluster in angry groups and taunt the officers from behind the tape. One of the TV station teams had arrived and was already setting up its periscope. Fitzgerald needed to call the station commander, brief him rapidly and then get a PIO out to the scene to handle the media, along with the Officer Involved Shooting Team from headquarters. Neither of the officers had been injured; that was fortunate—and amazing. Both appeared to be doing O.K. It was beginning to look like a righteous shooting.

Fitzgerald was just starting to feel a little better when a bearded mid eastern male wearing a white turban and a short sleeve blue Arco shirt walked up to him. He nodded slightly.

"Not to worry, my friend," he smiled, pointing to a small camera mounted on the Arco sign high above the parking lot. "Ahmad has recorded everything."

River Bottom Rum

HARMONICA JOE SAT on a small camp stool at the top of the ramp as the cars shot off the freeway and pulled into the left turn lane. A sign reading "homeless musisun God bless" was propped against a small wicker basket. Off to the side he had parked his bicycle with a flat rear tire which resembled an overloaded pack burro. Each side had green canvas saddle bags loaded with the essentials of homelessness. Bottles of water, a roll of toilet paper, a small plastic bag with a collection of half smoked cigarettes, a four by six blue vinyl tarp, a small umbrella and a worn King James Bible; four pairs of sunglasses and a pair of rubber goggles, an aluminum dog dish, a small flashlight, a TV remote, a claw hammer Red had given him for protection, and a blanket stuffed into a wire basket attached to the front handlebars. Inside the basket slept a small terrier, a mutt of some kind, twenty pounds or so, which looked like a piece of old shag carpet. Stan, he called him. The whole rig was complimented by a tattered American flag taped to the basket which stood up like a national semaphore demonstrating that even the homeless were patriotic.

Joe was buttoned into an old olive drab Army jacket, wore a leather aviator cap, and shuffled in untied, black high top tennis shoes. He wore rabbit fur lined gloves with the fingers cut out at the second knuckle. His pants had taken on that shiny leathery look they get from unwashed dirt and sweat and grime. If you asked him, he probably couldn't remember the last time he'd taken them off. He had learned a long time ago about the importance of eye contact when begging and how it could create guilt and produce a donation. So he deliberately stared hard at all the drivers when they stopped next to him. Problem was, his appearance and his deteriorating eye cataracts made him look dangerous and crazy. And he was crazy. He was a paranoid schizophrenic who had been hospitalized for more years than he could remember, talking back to those voices for so long they'd become old friends. He could recall the electroshock therapy and sometimes talked about it, but there were days when it appeared that he hadn't escaped the lobotomy experiments either. Nothing much had worked and when the state budget cut funding for psychiatric hospitals Harmonica Joe had been released with a handful of pills and the best wishes of the staff. He had managed to exist in his own world for the last few years with his music, and with Stan, his confidant.

He held a Sony harmonica in his hand and he could play anything if anyone had asked. But he pretty much stuck to the blues while sitting next to the freeway. He thought the blues encouraged giving. But he'd only collected a couple dollars for the day so he paid attention when a shiny white SUV pulled up next to the curb. The tinted driver's window rolled halfway down and a hand pushed out the window holding a bill.

"Hey, over here", a man's voice called out.

Joe stood up and walked slowly over to the SUV. The glass in the window gradually disappeared and he noticed a man with a pretty woman sitting next to him. He approached the window with his hand out, and as he did so the man leaned towards him, and spit in his face.

"Go fuck yourself, you old nigger", he yelled. Joe heard the woman laughing as the light changed and the man gunned the SUV around the corner.

He stood rigid, transfixed, as if he had been struck by a brain aneurism. For several minutes the cars pulling up the ramp slowed to look at the old black man standing motionless in the turn lane. They drove around him carefully, wondering what he was doing, if he had been hurt, or expecting him to do something suddenly. Eventually, Joe reached up and carefully wiped the spittle off his face with the back of his glove. He turned around, shuffled back to his bicycle, and petted the dog still sleeping in the blanket.

"It's good you didn't see that Stan. It woulda embarrass both of us. We isn't asking much are we buddy, and we still gets disrespected."

He sat down on the stool with his back to the traffic, put his harmonica to his lips, and began the first bars of "Jesus, Help this Sinner". After awhile, he put down the harmonica, tilted his head back, and laughed insanely for several minutes. Then he waved the others away, shut the door, turned the lock, and settled into his own silence and safety. It was good to be back home again where they couldn't get to him. His head dropped to his chest as his brain powered down into neurological neutral.

No one stopped to throw a bill in his basket. After an hour Harmonica Joe stood up, slowly gathered his things, and walked off pushing his bicycle with the flat rear tire. Stan stood up front in the basket barking at everyone like the Viking he wasn't.

B obby and Stretch walked parallel up and down the rows of cars parked in the shopping center casually looking inside each vehicle. Laptops, iPods, cell phones, briefcases, purses with credit cards. Stretch stopped, and gave Bobby a slight head nod at a silver Nissan Altima. Then she continued on a half dozen spaces and took her place leaning against the tailgate of a pickup. Bobby hustled over to the Altima and saw the laptop on the rear floor. He looked around quickly, made sure Stretch was ready, and then pulled a small steel punch from his jeans pocket. Another quick look and he noticed a Hispanic male coming down the row of cars. Dark pants, white shirt with tie, this was no homie. He could even be the driver of the Altima. He nodded to Stretch and headed away from the car. Four car lengths away from the Altima Stretch came around from behind the pickup and almost bumped into the guy.

"Whoa, excuse me", she smiled, "Do you know where Gina's Fashions is?"

The guy looked at her and hesitated. "No, what's Gina's Fashions?" He liked what he saw. Tall blonde, late twenties, tight jeans and heels, a little light in the chest but a great ass. Nicely packaged with a raspy Tanya Tucker voice.

"It's women's clothes," she laughed, "You probably wouldn't be familiar. I thought it was in the mall here." She gradually turned him around and wandered slowly towards the mall verbally dragging him along.

Bobby cautiously returned to the Altima, listening to Stretch keep his attention with talk about Abercrombie's and men's fashions. When they were out of earshot, he pulled the punch and with a single blow shattered the side passenger window. Tapping the lock, he opened the rear door and pulled out the laptop. A quick search of the glove box, console and under the front seat for anything else came up empty and he was gone. He quickly headed out of parking lot, found the bus bench around the corner and sat down to wait for Stretch.

Fifteen minutes later she jogged up. "Sorry, I couldn't get rid of the guy. He wanted to buy me a Starbucks, and when I turned him down, he asked for a blowjob. Can you believe that shit? What a pig."

"Yeah, well, fuck it. At least we got a laptop. Let's get over to Leon's and dump this thing."

Forty five minutes later they walked into Leon's Body Shop, carefully stepping around piles of greasy tools, car parts and tattooed fender men.

"Jesus, how can anyone work in a dump like this?" asked Stretch.

"Shut up, you'll piss him off,' cautioned Bobby. "Hey, where's Leon?" he shouted to anybody.

"Out back with a customer", someone yelled from underneath one of the cars.

They walked into Leon's office and Bobby sat down in his chair. He paged through the girlie mags he found in the drawer of the desk impatiently. Stretch refused to sit down on anything, lit a cigarette and leaned against the wall.

Leon finally walked in. "What the hell you got for me today, asshole?"

Bobby looked at this little old man and remembered how much he hated him. Balding, with a long gray goatee, braided with red, white and blue beads trailing under his chin. Permanent nose blackheads from life as a grease monkey. He was wearing a black sleeveless Harley T-shirt which showed off his aging tattoos. He brought the smell of motor oil and sweat into the room which made Bobby's eyes burn and felt like something infectious that would stick to clothes.

"Is that anyway to treat a customer?" asked Bobby.

"You ain't a customer. You're a pain in the ass. You never bring me anything but shit. And your line of credit been cancelled."

Bobby got pissed. "Look, Leon. I got a laptop, HP, probably worth six, seven hundred."

"Lemme see," he pushed Bobby out of his chair and opened the computer.

He played with it for a couple minutes and looked up. "Forty".

"You prick", screamed Bobby. "You know this thing's worth three, four hundred."

Leon laughed. "OK, fifty."

"Fuck you, Leon."

"Look man, what you gotta remember is that I gotta market for this shit . . . and you don't. So what you gonna do with this? Dump it off in a pawnshop? You willin' to run that risk? Have some dude give you up the minute the cops walk in the front door? Sell it on eBay? How about havin' a garage sale, dipshit?"

Bobby looked over at Stretch helplessly. She shrugged her shoulders and took a drag on her cigarette.

"OK, dammit. Gimme the fuckin' fifty."

Leon laughed and stood up to pull a handful of greasy bills from his pocket. He counted out fifty and dropped them on the desk. Bobby snatched them up and stalked out.

"Hey, baby", Leon called to Stretch as she turned to leave, "You ever dump this shit for brains and need a real man, you give me a ring, ya hear?"

She spun around and looked at him as if he had just licked the back of her neck.

The cowboy had been sitting in the stuffy VA office for over two hours waiting for his name to be called. He lounged comfortably half asleep in the chair having learned a long time ago to accept delay, confusion and indecision. After all, it took awhile for officers in the military to decide what to fuck up next. As far as he was concerned, if the shooting had stopped and there was no arterial bleeding there wasn't a crisis. Just another day in dogtown.

He looked around at his neighbors. Some were dressed in their cammies probably hoping they'd get better service if they wore their uniform. Others were accompanied by their wives, or girlfriends, probably there for family counseling. That was probably pretty interesting. Some of them without a babysitter had brought the kids along who crawled around on the dirty floor. An E-6 sergeant in uniform wore a TBI helmet, probably the victim of an IED. They varied in rank, age and assignments. But they shared one thing. They were the fucked up, walking wounded, suffering from PTSD. Post Traumatic Stress Disorder. Something the shrinks came up with after Vietnam. Recurrent nightmares. Temporary amnesia. Claustrophobia. Fear of strange noises. Lingering anxiety and depression. The cowboy would have added a smoldering anger. They shared the fear of being around strange people, driving on the freeways and loud noises. They couldn't sleep at night and used drugs and booze to numb the memories. They still heard the screaming of the dying, smelled the putrid stench of burning blood, and saw the faces of those who died in their arms. They were here for their fifty minute hour of weekly psychotherapy which the government generously provided to them free of charge.

"Sergeant Camacho", the receptionist finally called out.

"Sergeant Richard Camacho", she called out again with some added aggravation.

The cowboy shifted in his chair. He pulled out his iPod ear buds and tilted his head.

The receptionist stood up. "Is there a Sgt. Richard Camacho in the room?"

The cowboy stood up and walked to the receptionist. He was a little under six feet and about a hundred and seventy. He wore a blue denim shirt with the tails out over black jeans, boots and a black cowboy hat. He carried a backpack slung over one shoulder and he wore expensive

Panama Jack wraparound sunglasses. There was a slight hitch to his walk, as if he was getting ready to make a right turn.

"Dr. Hendricks", she said without looking up as he approached. "Room four, second door on your right."

The cowboy walked past her without saying anything and went down the hall. When he reached room four he stopped and stood in the doorway. A black man in a white coat with large horn rimmed glasses on his nose was studying a laptop computer.

"I'm Camacho", he finally said. The doctor looked up, seeming surprised.

"Oh, hi, have a seat. I'm Dr. Hendricks." He was small and wiry, engrossed in the computer. A narrow purple tie hung loosely under his prominent Adams's apple.

The cowboy sat down and dropped his backpack on the floor alongside him. He didn't remove his sunglasses.

The doctor finally looked up and pushed his glasses back.

"OK, Sergeant Camacho, I've reviewed your file. So how are you doing?"

The cowboy looked at him. "OK . . . I guess. What happened to Dr. Sanderson?"

"Oh, she's been transferred to another unit."

The cowboy leaned back, his disappointment showing. "I liked Dr. Sanderson. I felt like she was really helping me. She said we were doing some good work."

"Yeah, well, it was just a routine career move, you know. You've been assigned to me now and I'm sure we can work well together also." The doctor looked at him for some indication of agreement that didn't come. He hesitated before he spoke again.

"So how is the anxiety?"

"Seems a little better."

"Good . . . good. That represents progress. So the lithium and the Zoloft are working."

"I guess so." Although lately the cowboy thought maybe he ought to be carrying his lithium around in a Pez dispenser.

"And the nightmares?"

"Maybe not as often."

"Good, the Ambien and trazodone should help with that. And you're still going to group therapy?"

The cowboy hesitated. He had stopped attending the group sessions months ago when he realized how worthless it was for him to sit around with a bunch of lying mother fuckers bragging about their war heroics. Heroics, my ass, he thought. Just bullshit stories about them supposedly saving their buddies and killing hajjis. Bullshit. No, the cowboy had his own personal war stories as an Eleven Bravo. Light weapons infantry. He was one of those boots on the ground the Secretary of Defense was always talking about at the press conferences. The grunts with sand in their teeth and getting the pickled shit scared out of them a couple times a day. His memories were IED's disguised as junk alongside the road, pulling screaming guys without arms and legs out of a burning Humvee, and trying to comfort an Iraqi mother holding a child with its head blown off by a bomb the size of their house. No, these were his own carefully hoarded memories and they weren't for sharing.

"Yeah", he lied.

"And I notice you've been taking a small dose of Mellaril. How's that doing?"

"OK, I guess", he paused. "I can't remember what that's for."

The doctor raised an eyebrow. "It's a bit of a violence suppressant."

The cowboy looked at him impassively and shrugged his shoulders.

"OK, well then, I think we'll continue with these medications." He scribbled on a prescription pad and ripped off a script which he handed to the cowboy. He stood up and offered his hand.

"What about my appeal?"

The doctor looked confused. "Your appeal?"

"Yeah, my disability appeal."

He returned to the computer, tapped on it for several minutes and looked up. "It's still pending."

"Pending!" The cowboy stood up and took off his Panama Jack's. "My appeal has been pending for over nine months. I've got constant migraines, I can't sleep. I've lost most of the hearing in my left ear. I've still got nine pieces of shrapnel in my hip and shoulder. I've got colitis. I've been diagnosed with full blown PTSD, and I'm sick. I am FUCK—ING SICK! And I'm rated at only thirty five percent disability. When the hell are they going to do something about it?"

The doctor backed up a bit. "Well, it's just the system, you know, everything takes so long. It's really out of my control. It's all about administrative procedures. The military, you know."

The cowboy looked at the doctor and considered how easy it would be to kill him. Right here in his antiseptic office, wearing his horn rimmed glasses and his white fucking coat. A quick forearm to smash his larynx followed by a carotid choke. He'd be dead and history in thirty seconds.

The doctor fingered his Blackberry nervously as if he were expecting a call. The silence got through to him quickly. Twenty seconds, which seemed like an hour to the doctor, passed before the cowboy picked up his backpack and walked out.

The doctor sat down, a bit shaky. He reopened the computer and made an entry to increase the dosage of Mellaril for Sergeant Camacho.

The cowboy walked down the steps of the building, dodged the cars in the street and walked into the park, wandering a bit until he found an empty bench. He pulled a blunt out of his pack, lit it and settled back to take in the scene. Tattooed shirtless dirt bags sitting in a circle, hanging around to share dope and bullshit. A couple young girls eager to trade sex for dope on the fringe. The old blacks playing dominoes in the shade under the trees. And the dopers hanging around the restrooms with the perverts.

He watched a couple guys bartering a dope exchange. TARGET ACQUISITION. Seventy meters to his right, at two o'clock. A big guy, with a black lab puppy on a leash, and a skinny little shit wearing a white T-shirt like a headdress hanging down his back. The Iraqi bazaar coming to America, thought the cowboy. He watched them argue. TARGET SELECTION. He decided he would take out the skinny guy first. He had a jerky, nervousness about him that always spelled trouble. Unpredictable. The big guy would move slower. ENGAGEMENT OF MULTIPLE TARGETS. SIGHT ALIGNMENT. Breathe. Hold. SQUEEZE trigger. MOVE immediately. Hit and run. ESCAPE AND EVASION. SURVIVAL. Army Field Manual 23-10. Sniper Training and Operations.

He felt exposed and uneasy without his weapons. The cowboy had found that he was comfortable with weapons and he had become proficient with the SAW, a light machine gun that had replaced the heavier M-60 used by the infantry in Vietnam. At twenty two pounds of brute force it was a bastard to carry but made up for it when the shit hit the fan. He loved the sound of 750 furious rounds per minute, the feel of the stock hammering into his shoulder, and the smell of burnt gunpowder. It made him feel alive like never before; every nerve vibrating. He understood the necessity of violence, righteous violence, and he had easily accepted his role in carrying it out. That war was about killing people and destroying things. A hundred years ago he would have been the town square hangman. He also accepted the political theory that every ten or fifteen years an American president had to pick on some country and kick the shit out of them just to show who was still running the world. Who had the biggest dick on the block. He had displayed a coolness under the stress of combat that had surprised even him. And although the troops admired him, his platoon leader was concerned about his lack of emotion. But for the military he was a poster boy. Just as the assembly line of General Motors produced a new and improved driving machine every year, Camacho had come off the military assembly line a very efficient and effective killing machine.

After watching the two dopers complete the exchange and wander off in opposite directions he stood up and stretched. He hung out for another half hour and then, as a brilliant bronze sun reluctantly sank into the ocean and the air took on a damp chill, the cowboy picked up his backpack and started the hump down to the river bottom.

T en miles way in a frost colored Infinity in the rear parking lot of the Blue Lizard, Jasmine sat up and wiped off her mouth.

"There now honey, that wasn't so bad, was it?" she purred.

Tall and flat bellied, with short spunky hair and mocha colored skin, legs all the way up to her ass and a smoky voice, Jasmine could have been mistaken for a young actress. Unfortunately, she was a crack whore.

And since a stroke had left her with a slight limp, a droopy eyelid, and periodic seizures, her retail value had been reduced a bit lately.

The guy was about forty, well over six feet and about two hundred and a quarter, wearing black polyester slacks and a yellow Hawaiian shirt. He straightened his pants, pushed open the door and slid out of the car. He walked around to her side, opened the door, and clamped onto her right arm with his left. That was about when Jasmine realized she had seriously fucked up. He had scared her a bit when he first pulled over, but she needed the money and she craved the crack and so she had ignored her instincts. He jerked her out of the car and drove his fist into her midsection forcing her to bend over like a rag doll. He followed that with a knee to her face which slammed her back up against the roof of the car. And then he finished her off with a completely unnecessary right to her left temple. He let her slide down beside the car, stared at her for a moment, and then dragged her ninety eight pounds behind the dumpster in the rear of the parking lot. Without hurrying, he walked back to the car, climbed in and turned the key. He drove slowly out of the lot without looking back.

Jasmine lay on her side breathing shallowly, choking on teeth and blood. She wondered if she was still alive. Then a warm darkness enveloped her and her eyes slowly slid shut.

Red sat in the shade on the side of the clearing replacing the duct tape on the arms of his LaZboy. Out of the corner of his eye he watched Bobby and Stretch lying in a vinyl chaise lounge giggling while they shared a pipe. He marveled at how much effort the two blister-lipped zombies put into being worthless. Their whole life seemed to be a relentless search for meth like a couple of hungry coyotes running down a rabbit. Both were constantly wasted. Bobby's health had gone to shit with his loss of appetite and he'd developed the restlessness of the meth head. His eyes had become those of a cornered squirrel, that scary, desperate look for survival. Felony eyes, the cops called them. Stretch had lost her curves and constant scratching at the imaginary bugs under her skin had left her with open sores on her arms and legs. She looked like she hadn't eaten more than Top Ramen for a week. She smoked incessantly with the unconscious repetition of someone who had picked up the habit in the fifth or sixth grade. Lately, she'd taken on the vapid look of a weary pole dancer working too many hours. And her old man was supposedly a NASA engineer who had worked on the space shuttle or some shit. Bet he was proud of his little daughter now, thought Red.

He refocused his attention on wrapping the tape around the arms and waited for them to disappear into their tent. Before long they'd be crawling all over each other wailing away like a couple bobcats on fire. Sometimes they'd keep everybody up half the night. Red shook his head, polished off his beer and flipped the can into the pile he'd been building alongside his chair.

He looked up quickly hearing the dead arundo crack with the approach of someone. Surrounded by the thick stalks of cane and six foot cattails, it was impossible to enter the encampment without sounding like a runaway Clydesdale. But it provided a natural barrier and an early warning device that made Red and the cowboy comfortable. No one was going to surprise them.

"Yo, Red", Cowboy called out as he came down the parched and dusty trail to the clearing. The water had tired of crawling down to the river bottom a long time ago.

"Hey dude, so what did the U-nited States government do for its war hero today? They double your disability check?" Red asked with a grin. He had a gravel voice like the guy selling pickup trucks on TV.

The cowboy laughed. "Same old shit, same drugs, and my fucking appeal is still pending. New doctor, but the same old shit. Nothin' ever changes."

"Well, let me ease the pain a bit with a little river bottom rum, my friend. I got a couple bottles of King Cobra left over from last night."

The cowboy nodded and looked across the clearing at Bobby and Stretch who were beginning to pay more attention to each other.

Red got up and limped into his hut, which was an actual teepee. If it had been a house it would have been labeled a total trash-out. Years ago he had worked as an extra in a cowboys and Indians movie with Kevin Costner and had talked him out of one of the teepees used in the movie. It was held together by nothing but memories and he'd painted his own American Indian symbols all over it. It was special and everyone knew he'd die in it before he'd give it up. It also served as the focal point for the encampment and the informal dispute resolution meetings which were held in front at the picnic table. Inside Red had built a plywood bed to keep him off the ground away from the snakes and the spiders, and he had a huge framed picture of Jesus, the one in profile with a beard and long hair looking a little too sweet, propped up behind the bed.

He came back with a can of the malt liquor for each of them and handed one to the cowboy who took a swallow and grimaced.

"Shit. This stuff would be a helluva lot better if it was cold, Red".

"Yeah, well, sorry. This ain't the fuckin' Marriott. At least it's better than pruno."

"That's for damn sure. Apples were the worst. Damn, I hated the apples. Peaches were the best. But the smell of that fermentation in an eight by ten cell for two fools could really get through to you after awhile. I never did develop a taste for that shit."

"Me neither, and I never developed a taste for the joint either." They both laughed.

The cowboy looked over at Red and thought about the history of this man. From the wastelands of the reservation in South Dakota and the swamps of Vietnam to the empty halls of the Bureau of Indian Affairs and the smoky Indian casinos. He'd come of age in the barroom brawls and blood caked walls of the county jail, behind the barbed wire and steel bars of the state prison. The doctors estimated that with his alcoholism he'd probably been working on wet brain since he was a teenager. They also said he would have died years ago if it weren't for the fact that his kidneys seemed to function better than the radiator of a Peterbilt eighteen wheeler chugging up the Grapevine from Bakersfield. His pitted face, red as a monkey's ass, resembled a map of Los Angeles with its broken blood vessels in red and blue. Which is where he'd picked up his nickname, of course. Red had, as they say, a face made for radio. His real name on the police booking forms was Leonard Starts Fires. He was born in 1943 in Porcupine, South Dakota, and he was as Native American Indian as loincloth and firewater. He was missing a couple teeth in front from a disagreement here or there and he had a bit of a walleye from an old knife wound which gave you a choice of either eye to look at when you talked to him. Black hair as shiny as motor oil braided in a single strand slid down the center of his back. It was no wonder, thought the cowboy, that Red had become the Renaissance man for the homeless of the river bottom.

"Hey, Joe", Red called out to Harmonica Joe as he pushed his bike into the clearing.

"C'mon over, we got some river bottom rum for ya.' I got some new socks too. The guy from the mission stopped by this morning . . . dropped 'em off."

Joe lifted Stan out of the basket and unloaded his saddle bags without responding to the invitation. Red and the cowboy watched as he wandered around his lean-to. Within a few minutes he had reappeared and set up a jerry-rigged Hibachi grill out in front. He started a fire, opened a small can of dog food and placed it on the grill while Stan watched patiently. With a gloved hand, he turned the can and stirred the contents with a wooden spoon. After a few minutes, he pulled the can off the fire and set it down to cool. Periodically, he tasted the food, eventually deciding it was cool enough for Stan. He poured some of the food into Stan's dish, and then finished off the can with his spoon. Red called out to him again, but Joe paid no attention. Stan methodically cleaned his dish before wandering to the side of the clearing and relieving himself on a nearby bush. He immediately sat down, licked his genitals to the amusement of Red and the cowboy, and then disappeared into the lean-to. Minutes later, Joe got his Coleman lantern lit and the mournful sounds of his harmonica floated into the encampment.

"You know", Red mused, "I used to feel sorry for Joe, but sometimes I think he's better off than the rest of us. Ya got nothin', ya got nothin' to lose."

"'cept that dog. His whole life is that damn dog", added the cowboy.

"And his traveling." Red laughed.

Right. Harmonica Joe, the Time Traveler. He claimed he'd taken a trip to Mars on a black ops space ship with the Reverend Al Sharpton and Donald Trump a few years ago. He said Mars was pretty much a disappointment although they did find an empty bottle of Stolichnaya. He also claimed to have seen Elvis working downtown at the Jiffy Lube on 4th Street. This from a guy who claimed to have seen the inside of every psychiatric hospital in Southern California.

"Hey, we got a new arrival today, probably a parolee", Red remembered. "Wearing an ankle bracelet. A very unfriendly dude. Set up a new tent over behind Jasmine's. Didn't say a damn thing to me. I wondered if you could check on him tomorrow. You gonna be around?"

"Yeah, OK. I'll pay him a visit."

"Thanks, I'm gonna stop by the Indian Cultural Center and then hit the soup kitchen for some supplies. I'm still looking for a winter jacket." The cowboy nodded.

They drank deep into the night watching the campfires around them gradually die down. When the bottle of rum was empty and they'd smoked their last joint, they finished the night sharing a bottle of sweet cooking sherry. Neither one said much to the other for the last hour or so.

F ive hundred yards north of Red and the cowboy Matthew Markham leaned on the balcony railing of his room on the eighteenth floor of the Seaport Marina Suites and looked out over the Pacific Ocean. He watched the lights of a freighter slowly disappear into the darkness as he swirled the Courvoisier around in a large glass. He smiled to himself and looked over his shoulder at the voluptuous naked body curled up in the sheets on the bed. It had been one of those special afternoons. Hours of incessant and acrobatic sex, enough even for Matthew, who was a very difficult man to satisfy. The Chateaubriand for two, the Chilean wine and the Italian gelato had never tasted better. He'd take another run at her again and then scramble to the airport in the morning. He'd be back in Dallas and home with the family by late afternoon. Yes, life was good for Matthew Markham. He walked back into the room, dropped his terrycloth robe on the floor and tickled a foot poking out from under the sheets.

T he cowboy awoke to the smells of a dying fire and the burnt coffee Red had left for him. He poked his head out of the tent and looked around. The clearing was deserted and the fire was struggling to smolder. He pulled the flap shut and tied it. He unpacked his uniform jacket, spread it on his cot and smoothed it out before wiping off the medals with a sock. He straightened them carefully. The 82nd Airborne presidential unit citations, his jump wings, the Good Conduct and Middle Eastern Campaign Medals, his Combat Infantry Badge with wreath, an Army Commendation Medal, a purple heart with three stars, and the bronze star with a V. Then he opened his foot locker and pulled a small silver revolver from under the clothes and personal effects. He thumbed the cylinder release and dropped six rounds into his palm. He rolled the bullets in his hand slowly, inspecting each one carefully. He finally selected one and then methodically lined up the other five on the upper right shoulder of his uniform. Sitting down on his foot locker, he inserted the remaining bullet into the cylinder, spun it, and then clicked it shut. Putting his head down he paused for a full minute; then he straightened up, put the gun into his right ear and pulled the trigger. The hammer dropped with a cold metallic snap. He sighed deeply and his eyes remained closed as his head sunk down on his chest. Several minutes passed before he finally stood and picked up the other rounds from his uniform. He flipped open the cylinder, loaded the other five, and then returned the gun to his foot locker. Minutes later, he had covered his uniform with plastic and hung it back up in a corner of his tent.

The cowboy popped open a warm beer, swallowed a handful of pills and fell into Red's chair to wait for the rest of the day to go away.

S tretch stood at the coffee machine in the 7-Eleven stuffing a half dozen Slim Jims into the waistband of her jeans while Bobby bullshit questioned the clerk over at the coolers about the date stamp on a carton of milk for his baby. They had separated and she had come into the store a few minutes after Bobby so the clerk wouldn't connect the two. He may have suspected something but the guy conveniently ignored her while Bobby bothered him. She hung around the magazine rack at the front of the store for a minute and then hauled ass out the door. A few minutes later Bobby joined her on the bench in front of the car wash where they shared the Slim Jims and a quart of whole milk that Bobby was forced to buy.

"I'm going over to my sister's apartment this afternoon", announced Stretch. "She offered me a bubble bath and I'm going to be a pretty woman for a couple hours today. I'm gonna I'll stop by the car and pick up some clothes too. Clean up my act a bit."

Bobby lit a cigarette and blew a smoke ring that drifted by her face.

"Whatever. I'm going down to the methadone clinic, see who's around . . . what's available. And Luis was supposed to bring down a load of Humboldt weed over the weekend. That would be cool. I'll see what I can find."

Stretch laughed. "You go get 'im, honey. See you later tonight." She walked away leaving Bobby sitting on the bench eyeing the open door of an unoccupied Lexis waiting for the finishing touches of the car wash.

S ometime around noon the cowboy walked over to the new tent that had appeared behind Jasmine's. He carried a couple beers.

"Yo, neighbor", he called out as he approached.

He waited, considering a second greeting, when the tent flap suddenly opened and he walked out. Anglo, early thirties, wearing jeans and a black wife beater. Short spiky blond hair, earring in each ear, and a small goatee like a monkey boy. The usual tats on Gold's Gym biceps; not the hammers of a working man. The cowboy disliked him instantly.

"Hey, they call me Cowboy and I'm like the welcoming committee around here. So what's up with you?" He held out a beer to him, but he made no effort to take it.

"None of your fucking business."

"Look, I'm not trying to jump in your shit. I'm just asking where you're coming from."

"Where I'm coming from ain't none of your fucking business."

The cowboy looked at him curiously, realizing this was going downhill fast.

"You know, a while back parole brought a child molester down here. Couldn't find anyplace for him to stay. Created a lot of negative publicity.

No one wanted him around. It didn't work out. For him. Or us. He had an ankle bracelet and an attitude like you. You a child molester, dude?"

He snorted and took a step towards the cowboy. "Watch your fucking mouth, pardner. I ain't no child molester." The words spewed out of his mouth like molten lava.

The cowboy stood his ground and stared at him intently. He was shorter than the cowboy but more muscular and he had that look in his eye. He took an invasive step closer. The cowboy held out one of the beers, instinctively holding the other at his side like a grenade.

The cowboy waited for him, knowing it was coming. When it did he started with a left hook which was surprising but the cowboy slipped it easily. They traded a couple jabs and ineffective head blows before the cowboy took him down. He was a much better ground fighter and he quickly rolled him over onto his stomach with an arm bar. He broke his nose the third or fourth time he smashed his face into the ground and punished him with a series of elbow blows to his face. When he continued to resist the cowboy put him to sleep with a carotid choke. After he was finished he stood up and looked down at him.

"Stay away from us, asshole. Next time I'll kill you."

The child molester lay on the ground for a few minutes waiting to regain his senses. He snorted the blood out of his nose and tongued his teeth to check the damage. Pissed and embarrassed, but he was no stranger to getting his ass kicked. He'd suffered enough in the joint at the hands of the sadistic prison guards as often as getting jumped by the black brothers periodically. With the dysfunctional pathology of his family in his early childhood he was no stranger to blood and violence. Locked in his bedroom waiting for his step father to come home to punish him for something his dopey mother had decided was a violation of the family rules and regulations. And then when he finally stomped in the front door, fueled by too many boilermakers at Shanahan's pub, he'd whip off his belt and beat his ass until it bled and the old man had worked up a sweat. And then just when he thought he couldn't stand anymore, he'd bend him over the bed like a double barreled shotgun, pull his pants down, and rape him, screaming that if he didn't goddam straighten up there was a whole lot more where this was coming from. This drugstore cowboy, he said to himself, was a goddam nothing.

It was almost noon by the time Stretch loped into the rear parking lot of the K-Mart and found the old maroon Hyundai hidden in the shade of the pepper trees. She was relieved to find the car still there and more surprised that it hadn't been stolen or stripped. They should have moved it weeks ago before it got towed, but Bobby just never seemed to have the money for the new starter it needed. She had reminded him that with wheels they could get the hell out of Dodge but he still continued to smoke up all of her dreams.

She popped the trunk and rifled through the pile of clothes. Many of them were still on hangers or in plastic bags with the bar coded price tags on them. She finally settled on a new pair of jeans, a mint green blouse with a butterfly embroidered on the shoulder, a package of new Jockeys, and a couple new bras. She almost forgot a bottle of shampoo, conditioner and body wash. She gathered her things, stuffed them into a grocery bag and slammed the trunk shut. A quick look around and she headed to the bus stop.

The Big Blue bus pulled up and Stretch waited her turn to climb the steps. She followed a long line of others who also seemed to be carrying everything they owned. Small children clung to their mothers like Velcro. She walked sideways down the aisle and slid into a window seat, putting her bag on her lap. Minutes later the bus lurched out from the curb and continued on its route like a lazy worm engorging itself on people and then excreting them every couple blocks. Stretch searched the faces of the riders as they got on and shuffled down the aisle. Tired and downcast. Their hopelessness and helplessness was as thick as the putrid air on the bus. They all silently radiated defeat and despair. Stretch found herself wondering how long she could keep running with Bobby before it would all end. Prison, an overdose, AIDS, maybe a gunshot. One way or another she thought, it wouldn't be painless. Like Bobby and his kidney.

A year ago he'd gotten behind in a dope debt and one night three guys from the other side of the valley broke into his motel room, tied him up and poured a quart of antifreeze down his throat. It was almost four hours later when she got back from the free clinic and found him comatose on the floor. He'd lost a kidney a week later and damn near died but he still couldn't kick the meth. With each stop of the bus the depression became more stifling. Like a blanket thrown over her head. Claustrophobic. She struggled to fight it off but it hung on like a migraine headache. The sad realization. These were her people. She was one of them.

She sat on the front steps of her sister's apartment patiently even though it had been over three hours. She was sure she had the right day and she had said it would be best in the afternoon. It wasn't like her sister to stand her up either, but Stretch was beginning to wonder. She had asked a neighbor to call her sister's cell, but when she came back and said no one answered Stretch didn't believe her. She had that look, like I'm lying and you know I'm lying and I know you know, but I hope you don't call me on it. She considered forcing a window, but somebody would probably call the cops and they'd find an old warrant or some other bullshit reason to hook her up and she'd spend the weekend in jail. So she just sat on the steps. Waiting. Thinking about that bubble bath.

And crying quietly into the bag of clothes on her lap.

The police sergeant carefully picked his way through the brittle bamboo towards the clearing making no attempt to be quiet. He was always careful not to surprise anyone in the encampment. Although he was a frequent visitor to the river bottom, the river rats were a private bunch of outcasts who didn't like surprises or official company. Most of them had something in their pockets they didn't want to share with the cops. And he figured since most of them were armed with some kind of weapon you could never be too careful. When he broke through into the clearing he noticed Red crouched over the picnic table stirring something in a large pot. A mangy brown dog sleeping on his side under the table opened his eyes and watched the policeman cautiously but didn't bother to move.

"Morning, Red", he called out loudly. He was followed by a beefy female officer who stood off to the side and said nothing. She wore light blue latex gloves and looked uncomfortable.

"Hey sarg, what's up?"

"Well, it's been awhile since I stopped in and we thought we'd say hello. This here is Officer Gunderson. Been on about three months."

Red looked over at the rookie and nodded. She looked like she'd be more comfortable waiting tables in a truck stop diner.

"Can I talk you into some stew and a cup of river bottom coffee?"

The sergeant laughed. "No thanks Red, last time I had a cup of that stuff I was awake for three days."

"It'll definitely put some hair on your chest and lead in your pencil, that's for sure. How about you?" He motioned to Officer Gunderson.

"Ah . . . thanks, but no. I don't think that's going to work for me. Think I'll stick to decaf", she smiled nervously and went back to inspecting her arms for ticks.

The sergeant took a step forward. "Look, Red, the reason we stopped by was to tell you Jasmine is in the hospital. Somebody beat the dog shit out of her a couple nights ago. Out behind the Blue Lizard. She's going to be OK, but she's got a concussion, and some broken ribs. Lost a couple teeth. We figure it was one of her johns. But she hasn't exactly been too cooperative."

"She's a crack whore, sarg, she knows the life. Someday she's going to run out of luck and we're gonna find her face down in the river."

"Yeah, well, she almost bought the farm this time. The night cleaning crew found her and got the paramedics over there before she stopped breathing."

"She's made a choice to live that way. She just can't give up the rock. But I ain't her old man, sarg, I can't tell her what to do."

The sergeant nodded. "Well, I just wanted to give you a heads up and tell you to go easy on her when she comes home. She's going to be hurting for a few days".

"Yep, OK, we'll take care of her. She's one of us. Thanks, sarg."

"I understand you got a new neighbor. Another parolee?"

Red's eyes narrowed. "He's an angry man with a lotta baggage and he's gonna be trouble for us. He already got into it with the cowboy."

"Yeah, well, parole is trying to find him a place. They may put him into one of the hourly motels. Or ship his ass out of the county which would be the best for us. But he's been designated a violent sexual predator so we've got to tell the public about him and as soon as we do they organize a protest march and force parole to move him again. Nobody wants a sexual predator living in their backyard. Especially after that maniac kidnapped that girl up north and held her in a tent in his backyard for eighteen years. A few years ago they rounded up a bunch of these guys and made 'em pitch a tent on the front lawn at San Quentin. It was a pretty good idea for about five minutes until the A.C.L.U. heard about it."

They both laughed.

"We'll keep an eye on him, sarg. And we'll look after Jasmine."

"Thank you, my friend. And hey, by the way, we're still looking for Crow. He been back around here lately?"

"Nah, Crow knows he damn near killed Lenny and he's got a warrant out. Stuck him six times, right? Attempt murder arguin' over a goddamn dog. Wasn't even his. No, Crow ain't coming around here again. He knows he'd be better off gettin' arrested than coming back to the river bottom. These people would probably stone his ass or hang him from the bridge. Everyone here liked Lenny."

The sergeant shook his head. "Now listen Red. You get word to me if you see or hear anything. Don't let any of these people do something stupid."

Red nodded.

The police sergeant shook his hand, turned to the rookie and motioned for them to leave. She turned and plodded back up the hill trying not to fall on her ass.

Harmonica Joe pushed his bike with the flat rear tire and saddle bags down the sidewalk and into the entrance of the shopping mall. Stan rode up front as usual. Joe looked around carefully and then set up alongside the exit to the main drag. The cars leaving the mall sat in a line waiting to turn left at the light. He propped up his bike and set out his basket and sign. He duplicated some of his activities but either he didn't notice or it didn't seem to bother him. He left Stan curled up next to the bike with his bowl of water nearby while Joe walked up and down the line of cars. He was dressed in his old Army coat but had chosen a worn "Park Ranger" baseball hat for the day. He wore his black high tops and fingerless gloves. He also wore a second pair of fatigue pants with a dried dog turd in one of the pockets as a surprise gift for any of the cops who patted him down for doing nothing like they did so often. He'd smiled and appropriately thanked Stan for his donation. After a couple hours he'd collected close to ten dollars. He considered walking over to

McDonald's to buy a happy meal for Stan but he felt lucky, like when he'd won that two dollar scratcher at the liquor store. So he stayed on working the row of cars.

He first noticed them at the rear of the line, as they gradually creeped forward. A huge white white pickup, something big enough to carry a piano or a pig or something. A muscular young white guy in long L.A. Lakers shorts stood in the back holding onto a large piece of furniture strapped down in the bed of the truck. He eyed Joe suspiciously. When they pulled closer, the driver looked over at him, pointed at his misspelled sign and yelled, "Hey, dumb shit, your momma make that sign for you?"

Joe ignored him and moved on down the line. As they moved abreast of his bike the guy in the bed of the truck suddenly jumped out, ran over to the bike and grabbed Stan's leash. He pulled him toward the truck and climbed back into the bed, yelling at the driver who gradually increased his speed. Stan, suddenly awakened and surprised, started to trot alongside the truck while the guy pulled on his leash. As the truck picked up speed he began to tire quickly and then lost his footing. The pickup pulled out into the street dragging Stan on his side. In the middle of the road the guy in the back threw the leash in the air with a laugh and the truck disappeared down the street heading for the freeway. Joe turned around just in time to see Stan dragged into the traffic. Horrified, he ran to the dog lying still in the middle of the street. Traffic had stopped on both sides.

He kneeled down and stared at Stan. He was bleeding from the mouth, his right hip had been sanded down to expose the white bone and one of his front paws was bent all wrong. The traffic that had stopped began to impatiently crawl around Joe kneeling down and caressing the dog. He didn't know if he should pick him up but he couldn't leave him in the middle of the street either. He got down close to his face. Stan's eyes were shut and he wasn't breathing. He's dead, thought Joe. Whimpering with pain he picked him up and slowly carried him back to his bike. He wrapped him in the blanket, sat down and talked to him quietly. After a few minutes Stan opened his eyes and began shaking. Overcome with relief, Joe began crying with joy. He was alive. The shaking went on for ten minutes more while he held him gently and sang to him softly. Gradually the shaking subsided while Joe continued to rock him like a baby and sing him lullabies. The line of cars continued past the old man holding something in a blanket and weeping. None slowed down or stopped.

Another hour passed before Joe finally stood and placed Stan in the front basket of the bike and covered his face with the blanket. Collapsing next to the bike he moaned the inconsolable anguish of a parent who has lost a child. Eventually he looked up and around for his basket, retrieved it and discovered it was empty. He looked around, but saw nothing and no one. With disbelief, he slipped the basket and his sign into one of the saddle bags and aimlessly pushed his bike down the sidewalk to nowhere.

J asmine limped out of Memorial Hospital with a pounding headache, a bottle of eight Vicodin pills and a twenty dollar bill given to her by a sympathetic nurse from the ICU.

She knew she ought to hustle back down to the river bottom and take it easy for a couple days but the twenty was burning a hole in her pocket. She had given up feeling sorry for herself so long ago that she didn't notice the effort it took to make it over to the park. By the time she got there she was sweating in all the usual places. Her face looked like it had been encased in Saran Wrap.

She scanned the park looking for a connection. The white boys hanging out on the grass, some old black people playing dominoes under the trees, mothers with kids over at the play sets with the child molesters hanging around trying to look inconspicuous. The dope dealers hanging around the restrooms. Wheelchair Boy in the middle of the circle profanely trading bullshit with the white boys. Running away from a drive-by of homies he'd taken one in the back and when he woke up in recovery he learned that nothing below his waist worked anymore. Since then he figured he had the right to verbally rip every female that walked by, graphically describing what he'd do to her if only his Johnson still worked. Jasmine shied away from the group and stopped a couple dealers but no one had anything to share. Until Virgil showed up, that is.

At six five and three hundred pounds, sporting a huge black beard, wearing a XXXL oversized African shirt and dragging that dumb ass pit bull, Virgil could stop a riot all by himself. Nobody fucked with Virgil. Even the cops were respectful.

"Virgil, hey dawg, whassup?" she called out to him as he walked towards her.

"Da fuck happened to you, girl?" he stared at her wide eyed.

"Ran into a little bad luck . . . an unhappy customer, if you can imagine any dude complaining about a blow job."

He looked at her closely. "Teeth too?"

"Yeah, I got me a couple broke ribs too. Some big white guy. Damn near killed me Virgil, left me for dead behind the Blue Lizard the other night. The sorry muthafucka."

"Jesus", said Virgil sympathetically.

"Look, man, I need a couple rocks."

"Gonna cost you, bitch," he said slipping back into character.

"I got a twenty, but I gotta pick up some stuff at the drug store. Girl stuff, ya know?"

"C'mon girl, you know I'm a fuckin' businessman."

"I got's me some Vicodin."

"Shee-it. How many?"

"Eight."

"They give you any Oxycontin?"

"Nah, just the Vicodin."

"Damn."

He motioned her over to an area near the restrooms tugging the pit bull along with them. The dog had a large red mouth which constantly drooled as if he was about to rip into something. Or someone. Jasmine made sure she kept Virgil between her and the dog. When they reached the wall concealing the entry into the restrooms Virgil pulled out a small Ziploc baggie with several white rocks. He showed it to her, then put it back in his pocket and laughed.

"Lemme see the Vicodin, girl".

Jasmine pulled out the bottle which Virgil immediately snatched out of her hand. He opened it, shook out the pills and examined each one carefully. Then he replaced them and stuffed the bottle into his pocket.

Jasmine reached out and grabbed his arm. "Please Virgil, c'mon man, gimme the fuckin' rocks", she begged.

He looked at her and laughed at this scrawny little whore missing a couple front teeth. Then he dug out the baggie and threw it to her.

"Get outa here, bitch, you and your bad karma be dangerous to ol' Virgil."

Jasmine didn't waste any more time with him. Within minutes she was hustling down to the river bottom hoping no one had stolen her pipe while she was in the hospital.

S tretch stood along the boulevard carefully watching the traffic. The night fog had arrived with a chill in the air and she shivered a bit. She was wearing a short black skirt, red sleeveless top and a ton of mascara and eye shadow. She perched on five inch CFM heels and carried a small silver purse holding lipstick, cigarettes, a Bic lighter, a key, and a condom. She had been out there for forty five minutes without a hit. Several had slowed down to look her over but no one had stopped. She was starting to doubt herself when a dark green Volvo station wagon slowed and then pulled over to the curb. She noticed it had driven past twice. The tinted passenger window rolled down and Stretch looked in at a white guy, about forty, wearing a light blue button down shirt, khakis, and glasses. Could have been a high school history teacher. He wore a huge luminous watch, the kind that shows the time in Shanghai and the ocean temperature in Malibu. It was too large for his wrist.

"What's happening?" he smiled nervously.

"Not much, dude, just been hangin' out here waitin' for ya."

He laughed. "You aren't a cop, are you?"

"Nah, I flunked the written."

He laughed again. "How much?"

"Depends on what you're interested in, honey."

He leaned closer to the window and lowered his voice as if he was afraid someone else was going to hear him. "A blow job?"

Well, OK, she thought. At least he's not a cop. A cop would have insisted on her first offering the prices on the menu.

"Lucky for you, that's on special tonight. Twenty nine, ninety five. No checks."

He gamely tried out his negotiation skills. "How about twenty?"

"Hey, this ain't a fuckin' garage sale, bucko. You in . . . or out?"

He hesitated, then leaned over and pushed the passenger door open. "OK, hop in."

Stretch slid into the car and immediately choked on his Old Spice. "Straight up the street here, on the right side, I got a room at the motel", she directed him.

He pulled out into the traffic and looked straight ahead, occasionally sneaking a sideways glance at her, like a fisherman with his line thrown back in the water but looking at the one he just hauled in. When they reached the motel, he turned into the driveway alongside the rooms which led to the parking lot in back.

Sensing his nervousness, she offered, "We can get it on out here if you want. Be a little quicker."

He slipped it into Park, looked around and then nodded. "Yeah, I guess this is OK."

He flipped the steering wheel up, unsnapped his seat belt and pulled his zipper down with short, chubby fingers. Stretch reached over and put her hand in his crotch. He turned towards her with a grin, which made it easier for Bobby to surprise him when he opened the driver's door. He looked to his left as the door opened and Bobby hit him in the face with the tire iron. He gave him another quick hit and then dragged him out of the car and onto the pavement where he kicked him in the head a few times. He would say later after four days in a coma that the last thing he could recall was gassing up at the 76 station at 9th and Broadway.

Stretch quickly riffled through the glove box, the console, and checked under the front seat for a gun. Bobby rolled him over, pulled out his billfold and removed the cash and the credit cards.

Within a minute they had abandoned the car and were running down the alley. They only stopped long enough for Stretch to kick off her heels and slip into the pair of bulky sweat pants, a hoodie and sandals that Bobby gave her. Two blocks down they came out of the alley holding hands like a romantic young couple on their way to the market—and listening for the sirens.

Red stretched out in his LaZboy and took a long pull on his beer. He and the cowboy looked across the clearing and watched Harmonica Joe sitting in front of his tent. He held Stan's body wrapped in a blanket on his lap and he rocked back and forth, moaning. Occasionally he'd break into a quiet song.

"I'm worried about him, dude, he hasn't moved since last night. He's just kept up the moaning. And he's got to do something with that body pretty soon. I offered to help him bury it but he waved me off."

The cowboy nodded silently. He had pulled up a beach chair and sat alongside Red.

"That dog was the only thing he cared about, Red. Only family he had."

"Yeah, we jus' gotta let him do what he's gotta do."

Red groaned and got up from his chair. He handed his joint over to the cowboy, dug around in a warped plastic cooler under the table and pulled out a bottle of Ron Rico. He twisted the cap off and poured three fingers in a plastic cup for each of them and returned to his chair. He held the bottle in one hand and his cup in the other to save him from having to get up again. His weight had dwindled considerably over the years since, as he proclaimed with a grin, he didn't see any point in mixing food with his meals anymore. His protruding belly gave away his alcoholism which he readily admitted without embarrassment. He had long ago accepted the bloodlines of his family and made no apologies for what he considered his genetic gift of appreciating alcohol. At least I'm a connoisseur of something, he'd say with a laugh. Red didn't worry much about anything he couldn't change.

"You talk to Jasmine?" asked the cowboy.

"Yeah, jus' for a minute though, when she got back. She really got her ass kicked."

He pulled a blue package of Bugler tobacco from his shirt pocket and expertly rolled a cigarette. It was a habit he'd developed in the joint and couldn't seem to shake. Rolling his own that is. Just tasted better than any of the R.J.Reynolds smokes, he said. Damn sight cheaper, too.

"She's gonna' die on the street, Red."

"Yeah, and I think she came home with a couple rocks, too. Means she's probably over there gettin' fucked up."

"She ain't ever going to change, Red. She keeps talking about getting those kids of hers back, but it ain't gonna happen while she's still wasted. CPS has probably sold 'em to the gypsies by now. Bet she hasn't seen them in a year."

Red shook his head. "She's as good as dead, right now. She's been killing herself for a long time."

They both drank silently for a few minutes.

"'member when she got them frostbit tits?" asked Red.

They both laughed at the memory. Several months ago Jasmine had shoplifted a couple frozen pork chops from the local carniceria and hid them in her bra. On her way out the door the manager caught her, dragged her back to the security office and called the cops who didn't show up for an hour. In the meantime the manager had to wait for them because no one dared to look in her bra. When Jasmine's boobs started to freeze and she couldn't stand it anymore she jumped up, threw the frozen pork chops at them and escaped out the back door. When she got back to the river bottom she came running over and asked Red how to treat frostbite. Red offered an old Native American remedy which required warm human saliva applied directly to the affected area but when the cowboy exploded in laughter she walked off in disgust. Apparently both boobs survived saving her career.

"So what's up with the child molester?" asked Red. "He been around lately?"

"Not since our fight ended in a first round TKO", laughed the cowboy. "He's been pretty scarce. Probably out somewhere looking for the Olsen twins or Miley Cyrus."

Red laughed. "Don't assume that asshole has forgotten that. He may come around sometime when you ain't lookin' and knock you upside the head. He may not have found a gun yet but you know for damn sure he's gonna be lookin' for some payback."

The cowboy nodded and finished off his drink.

"You ever think about leaving, Red? I mean, just picking up and moving on. Finding something else? Somethin' better."

"Nah, this is home for me. I fit in around here. That's a sad fuckin' thought ain't it? But it's true. These are my people. This is my tribe. I'm just an old alky living on borrowed time. Even the docs are amazed I'm still around. I'm a goddamn medical miracle. My body's shot to shit and decaying but I'm still breathin'. I probably got maggots going to work on my guts right now."

He grinned and took a breath.

"And I understand these people. I understand why they're still here. See, it's all about structure, my friend. These river rats don't have no structure. They got no one telling 'em what to do, how to do it and when to do it. All the shit society puts on you. Calendars and alarm clocks, marriage and divorce, paying all them bills, car insurance, diamond lanes on the freeway, seatbelts, stop lights, registered Democrats and Republicans. The IRS. And religion. Ain't nothin' creates more guilt and fear of Armageddon than organized religion. Ya know? All that shit that gives you heart attacks and makes people kill their own kids. These people got none of that. I mean, panhandling and petty theft ain't much of a career, but it don't take a college degree or a fuckin' license. These people ain't trying to be anything they ain't. And they don't have anybody tellin' them they're late, asking 'em where the hell they been, or where they going. They need this free range lifestyle."

He paused. "Didn't mean to lecture you, dude. Don't know what got into me."

"Probably about a quart of Puerto Rican firewater", the cowboy said making them both laugh.

"So what the hell are you doing here, Sergeant Camacho? Besides learning how to be a professional drunk. Haven't you done enough camping in your life already?"

The cowboy shrugged.

"Couldn't get along with the family after coming home. My girlfriend ran off. My old man yelling at me all day about being worthless. Nagging my ass about a job, accusing me of faking my injuries. I just got sick of it. So I walked out, stayed with my sister for awhile, but the nightmares and the booze and shit—she got sick of me, and I just faded out. Ended up sleeping in the park after my pickup got repossessed, and eventually landed here in felony flats. Fucked up like the rest of these river rats. Lately I feel like I'm a danger to everybody, though. I get pissed off real easy, man. I damn near killed that child molester the other day. There's a lot of anger inside me, Red. It's pretty scary."

Red tossed the empty bottle of rum onto the pile with the others and cracked open a beer for each of them.

The cowboy took a gulp and continued.

"Some days I wonder why the hell I'm still around. I mean, I lost five of my buddies over there in that fucked up sandbox. For what? Damn Iraqis didn't give a shit. When I got back, I felt so fucking guilty I decided to go and meet their families. Tell them what a hero their dead son or husband was, whether he was or not. But then I only made it to one of 'em. I just couldn't take it anymore. I felt so guilty being there. I was embarrassed to be alive. Can you believe that shit? Embarrassed to be alive! What the hell is that? Why me? I know they asked that when I walked out the door. Why my son? Why not this fool? I felt like I should have been dead. Sometimes I just feel dead. Like nothing matters anymore. That's when I started drinking . . . you know. Everyday. And it just got worse."

"That's the way I felt in the joint", Red said nodding. "When you can't feel nothin' anymore. It's like being dead. Dead in your head."

The cowboy got up to stir the fire a bit, and settled back into his chair. "I lost my soul in that war, Red. It did some baaad shit to me. Fucked me up, man. Someday God's gonna be askin' me a few questions about some of the shit I did over there, shit I can't forget . . . shit that won't go away."

He shook his head in frustration. "And then . . . there's other days I feel like it was the only place I belonged. Like I fit in. I really got off on the rush of a good firefight—the sights, the sounds, the smells. I mean, I know that's fucked up, but I was a good soldier, Red. I mean like killin' those hajjis didn't bother me none. It came easy for me. I don't know, man. But like at least I knew what to do over there. Life was simple. Real fuckin' basic. Just life and death. That's all you gotta worry about, man. Livin' and dyin'. And gettin' some, making those hajjis pay the price whenever we had the chance. It was a simple life, Red. Real fuckin' simple. And now I don't know what's gonna happen. I mean, how the fuck is this all gonna end?"

Red nodded silently in understanding and stretched out in the LaZboy as the cowboy droned on.

They continued drinking until both were totally shitfaced. It was well after midnight before the cowboy finally limped off to his tent leaving Red paralyzed in his chair.

B ehind the flap of her tent, Jasmine had burned up most of the crack from Virgil. The pain of her broken ribs was a distant memory and she had forgotten the throbbing in her mouth. She held the world in her hands at the tip of the flame torching her pipe. When the flint in her Bic lighter was spent she had lit a small candle to keep the pipe going. She packed the last rock into the pipe and heated it with the candle. The first couple drags did what they were supposed to do and she continued to drift lazily when suddenly her forehead was hit by a bolt of lightning. Electric, like the time she was Tasered in jail. She stiffened and dropped the pipe. The candle burned carelessly on her makeshift bed, slowly igniting it. She watched the flames grow, mesmerized by the beauty of the orange and red colors blending. Then her body collapsed like a boneless bag of hot spit and spilled onto the ground. Her mind dissolved into a puddle on the earthen floor and she lay helplessly watching the hungry flames beginning to eat into the rest of the tent. It isn't the blue tunnel, Jasmine thought, but damn, the colors sure are beautiful.

T wo days later the local newspaper reported that a fire of suspicious origin had started in the early morning hours in the river bottom encampment of the homeless. A fire department official reported that the fire rapidly spread to the surrounding area and completely destroyed the camp before fire fighting equipment could reach the scene. The bodies of three unidentified persons and that of a small animal were recovered in the debris. A police sergeant contacted at the scene stated that the number of homeless residing in the encampment is unknown to authorities. An investigation is continuing.

Recompense

HE MUSCLED THE late model silver Chrysler 300 with smoked windows into the parking lot and slid into a space under the trees. He pushed open the door, strode into The Coffee Connection, and took his place in line. It had become a force of habit for him and he enjoyed a quick shot of his favorite blend for the last couple miles before he hit the office.

Although he wasn't one to wait for anything or anyone, this morning Tyson Wentworth waited patiently. In two hours he had to endure another quarterly conference call with the Wall Street SOB's and fund managers trying to convince them that the company was fundamentally sound in spite of the fact that the stock estimates were going to be down eight cents a share for the quarter. He had often wondered why the hell he had taken the company public. Everyone looking over his shoulder criticizing everything he did, questioning his judgment and decisions. Always demanding a better P/E ratio. SEC audits. Fortunately he had found an outstanding CFO to handle the details. Tyson hated the details, which he found boring. He was the big picture man. The rainmaker. The one who made the deals. The one with the vision. And TMW had been very successful over the years at the hand of Tyson Wentworth. But for now, this morning he took the time to marvel at the attractive baristas who demonstrated an amazing patience with the hundreds of early morning coffee drinkers demanding exotic personalized ingredients. What ever happened to a simple hot cup of Joe, he thought.

When he reached the front of the line he ordered quickly, took the paper cup in one hand and dropped a five on the counter. He added a hit of half and half on the way out, capped it with a plastic lid and took a slurp as he headed back to his car.

He had just tripped the electronic door lock when the man walked out from behind a tree. He appeared to be one of the neighborhood homeless and he startled Wentworth.

"Hey, man. Spare a buck?"

"Nah, get outa here," Wentworth shot back.

The man moved closer to him. "C'mon man, you can spare a buck. Driving a monster car like this. Wearing that suit and tie and all. You're a big shot, right?"

Wentworth eyed him warily. He was white, less threatening than a black, but still somewhat intimidating. Scraggly mustache and beard, unkempt long hair in a pony tail hanging down the back of a sweat stained Oakland Raiders baseball hat. Intense brown eyes poked out from under dirty strands of hair in his face.

"Get the hell outa here", Wentworth snarled.

The man didn't move. In fact, he took another step closer and held out a filthy hand, yellow tobacco stained fingers. A putrid smell reached out for Wentworth.

"C'mon, big man. Give me something. You can afford it. C'mon man. You, Mr. Success." He smiled at Wentworth. His neglected teeth were beginning to brown.

"Look asshole, I've worked my butt off for everything I have. Nobody ever gave me a goddamn thing. What the hell are you doing out here, begging like this? You worthless piece of shit. You're a drag on society. My tax dollars support your worthless ass."

The man looked at him curiously. "What's with all this anger, man, and lecture bullshit? I just asked for a buck or two for a cup of coffee."

Feeling challenged, Wentworth put his cup of coffee on the trunk of his car and turned around. The man had moved forward and was standing directly behind him. Surprised and feeling threatened, Wentworth instinctively pushed him in the chest, forcing him back.

"What was that all about", asked the man. "I didn't do anything . . ."

Wentworth swung a hard right to the left temple of the man. He went down like he'd been hit by an ax handle. Wentworth stood there for a moment and stared at him lying at his feet. For a moment he felt a rush of elation, like an underdog prizefighter who had just decked the champion. It passed quickly when the man didn't move.

He leaned over and looked at him lying on his back. It didn't look like he was breathing. He bent down and stared at him closely. There was a small cut on the side of his forehead that was beginning to bleed. His eyes were open but spasmodic, and his body quivered a bit.

Wentworth looked around nervously. He noticed no one in the immediate vicinity and the man was partially hidden alongside his car. He bent down again and shook the man. He remained unresponsive. He stood up and looked around again. Then he opened the door of the Chrysler and slid into the driver's seat. He took another look at him and then backed out carefully scanning the parking lot as he left. He saw no one. Two minutes later his knees started shaking uncontrollably. It got so bad he had to pull over to the curb and slip it into Park. He put his palms over both knees and pushed down, trying to force the shaking to stop. Finally, after several minutes the adrenalin pump slowed, the shaking receded, and his breathing became more regular. Jesus, he thought. And it hadn't even been a fight.

B y the time he pulled into the company lot his anxiety had dissipated somewhat and he had recovered his composure. He parked in his designated space and hurried into the building. Saying nothing to the security guard he usually greeted at the kiosk he walked over to the elevator banks. He waited for a minute, and then suddenly realized that he had left his coffee cup on the trunk of his car. It became more disturbing the more he thought about it and by the time he walked into his office he was considering returning to the parking lot.

Inquiries by his secretary, however, and an early meeting with his CFO in preparation for the conference call diverted his attention and it wasn't until lunch that his thoughts returned to the incident. His hand was starting to hurt and his middle knuckle was swollen a bit. He would have felt better if it had been a fight. But it hadn't. He had just sucker punched him. An unarmed, homeless guy just asking for a two dollar cup of coffee.

He had suffered through the late morning conference call, referred several questions to his CFO, and lost interest long before it was over. Shortly after eleven Wentworth told his secretary that he was going to take an early lunch and hurried out of the building. He drove past the coffee shop parking lot looking for anything unusual. A group of people. Emergency personnel. Leftover yellow police barricade tape. He drove around the block and approached from the other direction. There was nothing. No sign of anything. Cautiously, but without slowing, he drove through the lot looking for his coffee cup but didn't find it. For the first time in a long time, he was beginning to worry about something. Which was a new experience for Tyson Wentworth. His wealth, status and power had served him well over the years. People didn't mess with Tyson Wentworth. No sir, he was a big man in this city, with an army of experts, financial wizards, attorneys, and if necessary, politicos behind his projects. Fighting Wentworth was going to cost you. And you were probably going to lose. Tyson Wentworth was, City Hall.

That night, he watched the TV news and tried to casually surf all the news channels without Lauren noticing his unusual interest. Nothing but the economic crisis and more bad business and financial news. Trust funds, mutual funds, home loans, international bank loans, Credit Suisse, the World Bank, the IMF. Everything was flatlining. And those sanctimonious Washington bastards sitting on their ass, papering up the stimulus package with pork projects for their fat friends, and flipping the finger to everyone else. Wentworth poured another vodka martini and wished he could forget about what had happened that morning. Fortunately Lauren was pre-occupied with planning another fund raiser and spent the evening in her office on the phone. He didn't feel like talking. After checking all the news channels at ten and again at eleven he went to bed and tossed most of the night. Several times during the night he found himself awake replaying the incident.

If only he had turned left instead of right, or right instead of left. If only he had driven straight to the office. If only he had just walked away from the guy. If only he had called 9-1-1 the minute he dropped him. What the hell had he done? By five he was awake, staring at the ceiling waiting for the sound of the newspaper thrown into the driveway. He was up and out into the driveway thirty seconds after he heard it land. He padded back into the kitchen, poured a cup of coffee and began leafing through the paper. Page one. International and national. Section two. Metro stuff. Business. Sports. Classifieds. Nothing. It'd be in Metro, probably, he thought.

He turned it over and started again when he saw it on page seven. Three sentences.

"Homeless man found unconscious in the parking lot of The Coffee Connection. Remains in intensive care at Central Memorial Hospital. Police attempting to identify man and determine cause of what appears to be a serious brain injury."

Wentworth read the article three times. Jesus! His mind reeled. He had cold-cocked an unarmed man. He'd left the scene. Were there witnesses? What could he be charged with? Assault? What if he dies? Murder? Certainly not murder. There was no intent. Manslaughter maybe. Aggravated assault. But he could plead self defense. He could make a case for that. Unless there were witnesses. But he'd fled the scene. Maybe he could go to jail. He remembered one of his friends who had hit a kid with his car up in Oakland a few years ago and had gone to jail for eighteen months. Wasn't even drunk. Just speeding.

He stood up and realized that his hands were shaking. He walked out onto the patio and sat down by the pool. He had to think this thing through, which was something Tyson Wentworth was good at. He had a special talent, others said about him. His ability to focus on all the options, objectively evaluate each, and then make a sound decision based on the facts. It was what separated him from others and what had made him so successful. To see through all the bullshit and focus on the facts. He had become a successful CEO and a pillar of the local business community with those attributes. This was just one more problem to solve, he told himself.

The first was the guy. If conscious, he could provide a description of Wentworth. But with a brain injury . . . He considered calling the hospital, but that could be considered suspicious, especially if they asked for him to identify himself. He could refuse of course, or give them a fake name. But what if they recorded all the calls. Especially since this was a crime. But did they know it was a crime? It didn't sound like it from reading the newspaper account. Were there any witnesses who could identify him? He hadn't seen any. Or his vehicle. Maybe he ought to dump it. No, too suspicious. The employees at the coffee shop! Maybe one of them could have seen it. But he hadn't seen anyone. Would the baristas remember him? Of course, they all knew him.

And cameras. Dammit! Everyone had cameras these days. He hadn't noticed any but he hadn't looked for any either. And his coffee cup left on the trunk. That was the most worrisome. Must have fallen off right at the scene. Surely the cops would have found it. With his fingerprints. He tried to remember if he'd ever been fingerprinted. Yes, in the Marine Corps. A hundred years ago. Would they still be on file? Of course. The FBI kept those things forever. Jesus! Wentworth's mind started to unravel catastrophically. He forced himself to sit still and focus on deep breathing to fight off a panic attack. He felt a pain in chest and he wondered if he was having a heart attack. He waited, trying to push back the fear he was feeling. His mind reeled.

When nothing happened after several minutes he got up and walked back into the kitchen. Thank God, Lauren was still in bed. No one had seen his display of confusion. And fear.

The next day and the next were a blur of replays, questions, wondering and worry for Wentworth. He went through the motions at the office, but found himself listless and preoccupied. He lost his focus. He let his CFO take the lead in the weekly financial meeting while he slumped into near catatonia. He had stolen his CFO from a venture capital firm that had slipped into neutral and the financial wizard had responded by jumping into TMW with a vengeance. He never tired, always had the numbers and possessed an uncanny ability to see around the financial corners. His anticipation of Wall Street financial moves and trends was amazing. When the price of bananas went up in Brazil, if an embassy was bombed in Africa, or a Chinese ship hijacked by Somali pirates, he knew what affect it would have on TMW. He had kept TMW and Tyson in the lead and steered them away from the failures of others on Wall Street. His compensation was bundled close to a million but Tyson considered him worth every penny. He was truly a boy wonder. He was a little concerned about the fact that he was in his late thirties, never married, and had never raised an eyebrow at any of the young vixens in the office. And he knew nothing about what he did on his own time, but what the hell, thought Tyson, don't ask, don't tell. He considered the acceptance of his alternate life style, if that's what it was, a public demonstration of joining the politically correct. Just as long as nothing blew up into a media embarrassment for TMW.

Wentworth had stayed away from The Coffee Connection, but wondered constantly about the condition of the guy in the hospital. He was pouring himself into the bottle in the evenings and he couldn't remember having a normal bowel movement since the incident.

T hursday, mid morning. Wentworth sat at his desk pouring over the plans for the new NorthWind MarketPlace. It still lacked a complete Environmental Impact Report (EIR) which was holding up any further movement on the project. These projects were all about pushing people in your direction, he always said. He always did his best to begin with finesse and logic and to point out what was in it for the others. But sometimes it failed, and that's when Tyson Wentworth turned to muscle and hard ball. He was one of the best political fixers who worked very effectively behind closed doors. That was when those who opposed him or those dragging their feet found out just how connected he was in this town. Yes, Tyson Wentworth was a force to be reckoned with.

Fran, his secretary, buzzed him.

"A detective David Martinez, from the police department, line two."
Wentworth's heart stopped. He stifled a gasp.

"He say what it's about?"

"No, refused to say. Said he needs to talk to you directly."

Wentworth looked at the blinking red light on the phone for a few seconds, took a deep breath and then picked it up.

"Hello."

"Mr. Wentworth?"

"Yes."

"This is Detective David Martinez, police department, major crimes bureau. We're investigating an attack on a homeless man behind The Coffee Connection at 7th Street and 3rd Avenue a few days ago."

Wentworth stopped breathing. Then he slowly sucked in a shallow breath. "OK, so how can I help you?" He felt like his lungs were glued together and he was drowning.

"Well, sir, we talked to the employees in the coffee shop and one of them said you often stop by the place in the morning. Probably around the time this guy was assaulted. I was wondering if you might have seen something."

Wentworth hesitated. "No, not really. I mean, I haven't been in there for a few days. When did you say this happened?"

"Four days ago. Probably around seven thirty, eight, in the morning. In the rear parking lot."

"No. I can't really remember seeing anything." He wondered if Martinez could hear his heart beating. He looked down and watched his tie beating to the rhythm of his heart.

"So you didn't see a homeless guy hanging around back there?"

"No. Didn't see anyone. If that was one of the days I stopped by. I can't really remember if I had come by there on the day in question." The bullshit answer enveloped him like a cloud of dust and he silently choked on it.

"Well, the employees we talked to were pretty sure you were there that morning, Mr. Wentworth," Martinez persisted.

Wentworth bit his lip, wondering if that was a subtle accusation. He hesitated, not wanting to argue with the detective and appear defensive. But he wasn't going to offer anything he didn't need to. He wondered if they had found his coffee cup.

Suddenly he blurted out, "So how's the guy doing?"

"He's still in a coma, pretty severe head injury. Major epidural hematoma caused by a traumatic brain injury. TBI, like the guys in Iraq, you know? They've drilled a couple holes in his skull to drain the blood and reduce the swelling, but his prognosis is not good. Even if he survives he may have significant neurological damage."

"So you haven't been able to talk to him, eh?" Wentworth frowned, wondering if he had gone too far.

"No, he's been unconscious since he was discovered. Well, look, if you think of anything, please give me a ring. I left my number with your secretary." He felt Martinez losing interest.

"Sure, of course, anything. Thanks, detective."

Wentworth put the phone down slowly. Dammit. He'd lied. Twice. Tried to deny being there. A weak attempt to distance himself. And he had denied seeing the guy. Witnesses! Cameras! Did they have cameras? Martinez hadn't mentioned cameras. What if they had the whole thing on tape? Was Martinez just looking for a denial before confronting him with the tape? No, if he had a tape, he would have walked in the front door of his office. No, they were still fishing. But the guy had been seriously injured, that much for sure.

Wentworth shuddered, wondering if he could survive any more police inquiries. He realized he was a novice at deception and he didn't like the feeling. He wasn't completely convinced Martinez had bought his story either.

Wentworth waved off a couple meetings in the afternoon and took a drive down the Pacific Coast Highway. Normally, PCH was a great stress reducer for Wentworth. A lazy drive. Turquoise water, bleached sands, blond sun and a constant ocean breeze pushing the sins of California into the wastelands of Nevada. Who couldn't love California? Even if the Terminator had fucked up the state budget worse than The Thin Man who had been recalled for the same failures. It was still the only place Tyson Wentworth could imagine living. There were just too many opportunities. Southern California still had the money for a developer like Wentworth. Today though, Wentworth was totally pre-occupied and appreciated none of the scenery. It was all about this damn homeless guy. And more importantly, it was all about Tyson Wentworth.

The next couple weeks passed for Wentworth and gradually took on a pattern. He began to lose interest in his construction projects, he had returned to medication again to force himself to sleep, and he was seriously abusing his liquor cabinet. His blood pressure rose, and his headaches returned. His golf game had become embarrassing. He developed a nervous quickness about him. Jittery. Like someone walking downstairs in the middle of the night to investigate a strange noise. He spent a lot of time sitting alone in front of the pool. Like he was waiting for the arrival of something.

An hour after dinner Lauren walked out to the patio and sat down beside him.

"Oh, Ty, you've gone back to cigarettes again also. What in the world is going on with you?"

She smiled at him wearily wondering what had happened to the man she had married. She had begun to worry about the coolness that had developed between them, like the draft from a leaky window. She had retained the looks of her early thirties, and those who didn't know them thought she was a trophy wife. That there was someone else he'd left behind years ago. In fact, she had been with him from the start, they'd met in college, and they had been married for twenty six years. She had borne him a beautiful daughter who had the movie star looks of her mother and a son who Tyson had been grooming to take over the business. Alexis was finishing her last year in law school and Alan had been interning at one of the best urban planning firms in the city for the last year. They had been a successful and happy family. They summered in the Hamptons and they wintered in Vail. Tyson Wentworth had provided well for his family.

"We haven't had a decent conversation in weeks, Ty. You're not eating well, you can't sleep without a pill, you're smoking again, and you're—I hate to say this because I don't want to start an argument—but you're drinking too much again. We haven't slept together in weeks. And Fran has told me you seem to have lost interest in your projects at work. What's going on with you?"

Tyson glanced at her briefly, shook his head and stared back at the pool. He punched out the cigarette. He knew it was useless to try to deny her description of his deterioration. She was right. He also knew he couldn't tell her what had happened. She probably figured he was having another affair. They'd weathered a couple of those over the years, and not without some painful counseling. But this was different.

Lauren doubted another affair. She had seen none of the signs she had become so tuned to notice. No, this was different. A business loss, a friendship, a lawsuit, he'd talk to her about. A health issue? No, something else was going on and she was just going to have to be patient and hold on. Like waiting for a fever to break.

Both sat in an awkward silence for a few minutes, trying to figure what to say to the other. After several minutes Lauren slowly wandered back into the kitchen. Tyson got up and fixed another drink.

W entworth's interest in the business continued to deteriorate. Each day he eagerly scanned the newspaper for an update on the homeless guy. Then one day he noticed an article regarding the Community Housing Project for the Homeless which had stalled due to cost overruns. When the community leaders had broken ground three years ago, the housing project had been billed as the west coast model for helping the homeless. The project was loaded with green enhancements which had attracted all the environmental proponents and "save the planet" wackos. A couple of obnoxious Hollywood celebrities had shown up, primarily to take advantage of the media coverage. One had even driven up in a Smart Car the color of money which had drawn as much interest as the project itself. Unfortunately, going green had been more costly than expected and the construction had stalled. It was a little south of three million short.

Wentworth turned to his laptop and pumped up the financials on the project. It didn't appear to have any significant below the line adjustments adversely affecting the completion costs. The construction company was well known to him as a reputable firm and he knew the general contractor personally. He carefully studied the building plans, construction proposals and costs, change orders, the EIR, the balance sheets and the accounting records for an hour. Then he called the project director at the city manager's office.

"John, Tyson Wentworth. I think I can help you with the Community Housing Project." Ten minutes later and the problem was solved. Once again, Tyson Wentworth had stepped up and come through for the community.

T yson lay semi-catatonic in front of his fifty-five inch Sony LED TV watching one of the cable talk shows. These things had become like human cock fights, he thought, with all the split screen participants screaming at each other. The moderator was talking about a homeless guy who had been set on fire down on Skid Row and the guests were a young police commander with a Jay Leno chin, a balding ACLU attorney with thick glasses and a greasy beard, and the director of a rescue mission wearing a light blue cardigan sweater with a stomach that challenged the buttons on the sweater.

"Who DOES this kind of thing", asked the moderator, somewhat rhetorically. "We've had homeless people shot, stabbed, beaten and now set on fire. What's with these hate crimes?"

"It's the young ruffians, Baxter, looking for a thrill," suggested the police commander. "Sometimes it's a gang initiation. Sometimes it's just human inhumanity. Worse than animals." He shook his head to demonstrate that he considered the acts incomprehensible.

"Well, a lot of these guys just haven't had a chance; they've been deprived of a normal home life", said the attorney. "Mom and dad are drug addicts, they were physically or sexually abused as kids, and they just haven't learned a normal morality. How to cope with life's pressures appropriately. In many ways, we as a society are responsible for these human failures."

"Well, nevertheless", Baxter interrupted, "This has got to stop. What kind of society do we live in where people kill the helpless? Where is the city council in this crisis? Why aren't we hearing from them? And the district attorney? Why aren't we prosecuting these hate crimes? To the fullest! What are we doing to prevent this from happening again?"

"We've reassigned several officers from Metro to the Skid Row area, Baxter," offered the police commander sounding helpful and hopeless at the same time. "We expect our increased police presence to reduce these incidents."

"Increased police enforcement isn't the answer, commander," lectured the attorney. "We need legislation to protect our homeless and to punish those preying on them. It's only going to get worse as the economic crisis produces more homeless people and families. And the children . . ."

"That's right, Baxter", chimed in the director of the rescue mission. "Our donations are dwindling. But we need more than donations. We need grant money for more beds at the mission, food and medical help. Adult occupational training and day care for the children. Maybe a half cent tax for welfare programs."

"Well", snorted Baxter, "I'm not sure the citizens of this fair city are ready for another tax. But we've definitely got to do a better job of protecting the homeless from the jackals out there. You've heard the expression", he wrinkled his forehead as he turned to face the camera, "You can judge a civilization on how well it takes care of those who can't take care of themselves."

"And for that we ought to be embarrassed," added the attorney

"So what I'd like to see is the police department and the DA's office start tracking these assaults against the homeless", responded Baxter. "Especially the mentally ill, who seem to be victimized the most often. Maybe with some facts and meaningful statistics we can come up with a solution to reduce the number of these incidents."

Baxter sat back in his chair and smiled smugly at the audience as if he had just solved the crisis in four minutes. "OK, let's go to our sponsors for a minute and pay some bills. We'll be right back with you with an interview of Councilwoman Sylvia Carson who has an educational proposal for increasing the S.A.T. scores for our high school students."

The TV screen went to a skinny blond pushing an ad for Jenny Craig.

Wentworth tapped on the remote and flipped over to ESPN. Then he got up and fixed another stiff one.

The night of the dinner, Tyson dressed early and went downstairs to fix a drink. Lauren poked around in her dressing room before finally settling on the right dress. Over the years Tyson had been recognized for many of his civic projects, his membership on various non-profit boards, and for many of his construction projects. But this dinner was special. Tonight he was going to be recognized by the Chamber of Commerce as the Man of the Year for his leadership and development of various civic projects, not the least of which was his donation of funds to complete the stalled Community Housing Project for the Homeless. He had bailed out the project and the head of every non-profit in the city would be present to personally thank Tyson for his unselfish efforts. Yes, thought Lauren, it was going to be a great evening.

Finally finished dressing, Lauren came down the stairs and found Tyson in the library, pouring a second drink. He was too preoccupied to notice that she looked gorgeous.

"It's going to be a great night, Ty, I can't wait", she gushed. He looked at her with a forced smile, and wished he could tell her the awful truth. It had been difficult, holding this thing in. The loneliness had been terrible. He had desperately tried to decline the award, but the president of the Chamber would hear none of it. No, he said, absolutely not. It was about time this city recognized Tyson Wentworth for the real man that he was.

An hour later the Man of the Year pulled under the main portico of the Four Seasons Hotel. The valets jumped at the silver Chrysler 300 ("Be American, buy American" Ty always said) and helped Lauren out of the vehicle. She took Tyson's arm and the two of them walked proudly into the hotel lobby like America's First Couple at a White House dinner. Actually the Wentworth's had visited the White House and slept in the Lincoln bedroom during the Bush years, a payback for Tyson's fundraising efforts for the RNC. Lauren had considered some of the décor outdated and Tyson thought the mattress needed to be replaced. But it had been memorable and they had entertained their friends back home recounting the experience. Along the way into the hotel they accepted the congratulations of the other guests and Lauren's graciousness overshadowed Tyson's tightlipped demeanor. Eventually, after a few drinks and the usual meaningless conversation, the attendees took their places at the tables for eight and forged their way through the rubber chicken, green beans and small talk before the speeches.

Tyson and Lauren patiently waited through the presentations and speeches of the other winners of various civic awards. The Educator of the Year had developed a teaching model to help high school minorities pass senior year algebra, the Red Cross volunteer of the Year, the Businesswoman of the Year who Tyson knew was eyeing the governor's office, the Most Promising Entrepreneur, an Asian of course, the chairwoman of the Prevention of Violence Against Women Foundation, the Police Officer of the Year for his work with gang members, and a group of eager young teenagers responsible for the most creative Green Civic Project which was some kind of solar driven well. The Woman of the Year was recognized for organizing a prison hospital action committee to improve medical care for inmates. Tyson struggled to stay interested. He had never wanted more to be somewhere else.

The President of the Chamber finally took the podium and smiled broadly at the audience as if he was going to pass out a new BMW to each of the attendees.

"Ladies and gentlemen, before we get started with our scheduled program, I would like to announce a surprise speaker tonight, Mr. Glen O'Brien. Glen O'Brien is an attorney from the Bay area. Glen is also the brother of Thomas O'Brien. And for those of you who are unfamiliar with him, I will tell you that Thomas O'Brien is a homeless man who was attacked and battered several weeks ago behind The Coffee Connection on the north side. Glen has been representing the homeless for several years and since we're honoring the Man of the Year for his participation in the Community Housing Project for the Homeless tonight, we thought Glen's remarks would blend in well with the others."

Tyson Wentworth felt the blood drain out of his face and a spasm in his lower colon.

"Ladies and gentlemen, please welcome Mr. Glen O'Brien."

As the applause died down, Glen O'Brien bounded up to the dais, took his place behind the podium and carefully adjusted the microphone. Wentworth, attempting to shield his shock, stared at O'Brien intently. He bore no resemblance to the homeless man he could recall from the rear parking lot of the coffee shop. His brother! Wentworth felt like a criminal defendant watching the jury solemnly file back into the courtroom with a guilty verdict. His heart began to pound and he felt like his lungs had collapsed. He was suffocating.

"Good evening, ladies and gentlemen. Thank you for this opportunity to speak to you tonight and to share a few things about my brother Tom. Yes, Tom was homeless. And yes, Tom was unemployed. And yes, Tom was an alcoholic and a drug user. Tom didn't make it easy for anyone. And that includes me. We begged him to come in, to come in off the streets, but he refused. He felt at home on the streets. You see, bad things happened to Tom, and he felt that he deserved to be homeless. Tom was a geneticist at UC Berkeley who was involved in the development of the human Genome. He was really . . . a brilliant scientist."

Wentworth listened carefully. He had begun to heat up and he worked to regulate his breathing. His stomach started to burn like an ember flaring up in a backyard barbecue.

Lauren beamed with interest and anticipation. She reached over for Tyson's hand and held it possessively. He didn't notice.

O'Brien continued.

"My brother Tom loved his wife Nora, but then a few years ago she developed ovarian cancer. And so he poured all his research efforts into finding a cure for ovarian cancer. But ultimately he was unsuccessful and after three years Nora died, a slow, painful death. And he grieved like you would expect of a man who loved his wife with every part of his soul. He became inconsolable. Part of him died with her."

Glen hesitated, looked out at the audience, took a deep breath and continued.

"Shortly thereafter, his daughter dropped out of college, drifted into the underworld of drugs and disappeared. And that's when Tom's drinking began to overcome him. His sadness was just overwhelming. He was completely and totally grief stricken. He had lost so much of his family. He became depressed, clinically depressed, but refused to take any medication. He said that medication just masked the pain, and actually prevented a cure. So he clung to his son, all that he had left, like a life raft."

"And then his son, a beautifully compassionate young man, on a journey to India with a church group, was killed while riding an overloaded bus which drove off a mountain road. And that was the end of life, a normal life, for Tom. After the funeral Tom just kind of dropped out. He sold his house, gave the contents to a non-profit, and moved into his car. Eventually he even abandoned the car and began living on the streets. I think he felt that if he didn't have anything, there wasn't anything more to lose. We feared suicide when he would disappear for months. But eventually, after many years, he became comfortable on the streets."

The audience had become still. Glen had them listening breathlessly. Some of the women were dabbing their eyes to prevent their makeup from running. Even the waiters had stopped cleaning up the tables and stood along the side of the room. The raspberry sherbet with a chocolate twirl was melting on the trays outside in the hallway.

"Since Tom's accident, or since suffering his injuries I should say, we have been planning to try to bring him out of his coma, with the hope that we could communicate with him. We have been working with the doctors, and we had planned to announce tonight that Tom had regained . . ."

Tyson Wentworth leaned over to Lauren, "Be back in a minute," he whispered. He stood up, kissed her gently on the back of the neck making her blush, and walked to the rear of the room. His flaming guts felt like they were going to implode. He pushed the door open and walked purposely through the lobby. As he reached the front doors of the hotel he sucked in a deep breath that sounded life saving.

He handed his ticket to the valet at the kiosk and said, "Gimme the keys. I need to get something out of my car." Handed the keys, he walked through the parking lot to the Chrysler and popped open the trunk.

Inside the hotel, Glen was finishing his remarks.

" . . . consciousness and was talking to us for the first time in months. And of course, we were hoping that he could tell us what happened to him. Maybe identify who had hurt him so badly. But unfortunately, my brother Tom succumbed to his injuries late this afternoon and died peacefully. Tom is finally at rest. Hopefully his demons have died with him."

Gasps from the crowd broke out and Glenn bowed his head. He took a minute to compose himself and to wait for the expressions of surprise and the hushed cries to die down in the audience.

"We thought my appearance and these remarks would be appropriate since we are honoring the Man of The Year for his civic contributions and his financial assistance to ensure the completion of the Community Housing Project for the Homeless. I just wanted you to know a little more about my brother. He wasn't a worthless homeless drag on society. He was just a man pushed over the edge. I loved him. And if you had known him you would have loved him too. Tom's organs were donated to several individuals whose lives will be saved now. Tom would have wanted it that way. I hope you understand."

He paused dramatically. "Thank you for your kind attention."

Glenn shook hands warmly with the chamber president and returned to his seat. The applause went on for a full two minutes and then gradually died down with people whispering to each other.

The president regained the podium, looked over to the Wentworth table and noticed Tyson missing. He looked inquiringly at Lauren who shook her head and spread her hands in her lap as if to say "I don't know where he is". He thanked the crowd again for its attendance and congratulated all the other winners to buy a little more time and then began the introduction.

"And now, ladies and gentlemen, our honored guest for the evening, our Chamber of Commerce Man of the Year. Tyson Wentworth is a native son who was born . . ."

Outside in the parking lot the two car valets jumped when they heard the gunshot. They were two witnesses who knew exactly what they had heard. They hadn't survived years in the barrio without recognizing the sound of danger. Knowing when to freeze and knowing when to run. Cautiously, both walked towards the Chrysler and carefully looked at the large man slumped against the rear bumper of the car. A large black .45 caliber semi-automatic was lying loosely in his right hand at his side. Blood splatters and brain matter covered the trunk. With the barrel of the gun apparently pressed to his right temple, when he pulled the trigger the top of his skull had disintegrated. What was left of his face hung loosely on his chin. Neither valet got too close to the man. One made the sign of the cross and turned to the other.

"Santo mierda. A llamar al 9-1-1."

The Letter

H E SAT DOWN on his bunk and looked at the envelope but failed to recognize the return address. He held it gently as if it was breakable and turned it over slowly. Then after a minute or so he slid his fingernail along the edge, opened it and slipped out a handwritten letter; four pages on lined yellow notebook paper. He read it slowly, as if he were placing a ruler under each line.

"I'm writing this letter to you because I'm dying and it's important for you to know that. I didn't want to write it but Alison insisted. So here it is. Life's been pretty miserable for a long time and a lot of bad things have happened to me. I've got a feeding tube in my stomach now. Actually for the last four months. The doctors have finally accepted my decision that I want to do this, and so they've just been trying to make life bearable. I'm supposed to feed myself from a high protein synthetic feed bag a couple times a day but I've reduced that to just once in the morning to speed up the process of dying.

I just pump it into a stomach shunt I have implanted in my side. But I've pretty much even stopped this and I'm down to 68 pounds. It's painful but a damn sight easier than the nasogastric tube they first tried to get me to use for a couple weeks before I went fucking crazy. It was way too much of a reminder. The doctors first thought I was just a simple case of anorexia nervosa, you know, with some congenital orneriness thrown in. But through therapy with Alison (I see her three or four times a week) the real reason for my problems had finally become apparent. After what you did to me, what you forced into my mouth, and after what you made me do with it, for all those years, it should come as no surprise to you that I can't put anything in my mouth. Including food. It's become repulsive. I'd rather die than put something in my mouth. And so that's what I'm doing.

I've come to a pretty rational decision that dying is better than going through this feed bag thing every day. I almost died from pancreatitis around Christmas and spent three weeks in ICU. My liver and kidneys have also been seriously affected by the loss of normal digestive functioning. I've suffered from fibromyalgia and osteoporosis. My bones hurt all the time and my knees and elbows have become somewhat deformed. Most of the time I have to use a wheelchair to get around. And the only thing that takes the edge off the internal organ pain is oxycontin, which is pretty heavy duty stuff. Makes me hallucinate too. The cognitive function of my brain has deteriorated and I can't seem to remember how to do some basic things anymore. Like sequencing of activities. Sometimes I try to put my socks on over my shoes. It's really been a drag lately.

I'm sending you this letter as one of the therapeutic steps to unburden myself of the awfulness you did to me. Alison says that it's an important step for the survivor to tell the abuser exactly, and graphically, how she feels. Actually, I really want this letter to hurt you. I want you to remember the rest of your life that the perverted things you did to me actually killed me. When I'm forced to go back and think about when it all started, I can't believe that anyone, especially you, could do that to a five year old girl. And that I couldn't escape you until I was almost sixteen! Sweet sixteen. All those years turned me into a freak. Sexual anorexia, the shrinks call it, with a sexual abuse etiology. My growing adolescence, puberty and developing sexuality were a complex and confusing mix of emotions. And I lost my normality along the way. I have never had a normal sexual experience with a man. Ever. You made men too threatening to me. Women are unappealing to me and I have no interest in trying that (I imagine in your perverted mind that you're probably wondering about that). I am totally afraid of them all becoming what you were, of forcing themselves on me like you did.

I tried to escape all those years, when you started abusing me. I tried to go to another place. A happy place. Or to become someone else. One of my teddy bears, or a Barbie doll. But it didn't work. I was helpless, unable to run. I can still feel all the pain. And the frustration that I couldn't stop you. I was powerless. You controlled me like a prisoner. Well, it's a little different now and I'm driving the bus today. You aren't here anymore and I'm the one in charge. And no one is going to change that.

I know you think that you've paid for your evil acts, that society has punished you enough. That your thirty nine year prison sentence and the abuse and assaults you suffer are enough payback. And the sex offender tag hanging around your neck like a target. But it isn't enough for me. You turned me into a freak. The shrinks have studied me like a rat in a transparent lab cage. Like I'm some kind of carnival act with two vaginas or something. And now you're killing me. I have no compassion or sympathy or forgiveness in me. I hate you.

The doctors estimate that I have about a month left before I suffer a cardiac arrest, a stroke, or total kidney failure. They have accepted my decision not to fight it. I carry a notarized DNR document with me at all times. Some of them think I'm crazy. Maybe so. Whatever. It doesn't matter anymore. My life is so over. I'm better off that way. Alison has promised to be there and hold my hand so I won't die alone.

You better remember what you did to me, you evil monster. You killed me."

Your daughter.

Military Briefs

S HE HAD HELD it together pretty well during the service until his friends got up to tell their stories about him. Then she came apart. And it only got worse. The eight-man color guard firing three volleys over the grave, the God awful mourning of Taps by the bugler, and finally the tri-folding of the flag which seemed to drag on forever. Everything at the military burial ceremony was agonizingly slow, dragged out as if the participants were dreading their next assignment. When the flag was finally folded and all that showed were the blue and the stars, the detail leader handed the flag with the triangle facing away from him to the sergeant and slowly saluted the flag. The sergeant made an about face, marched up to her and knelt on one knee. He put the flag in her hands but did not release it.

"Mr. and Mrs. Casey", he spoke in a commanding baritone, "On behalf of the President of the United States, the Secretary of the Army, and a grateful nation, please accept this flag as a symbol of our appreciation for the service of your loved one to God, country, and the United States Army. May God bless you."

He released the tri-folded flag to her which she gently placed on her lap. He straightened up, saluted very slowly, made an about face and marched to the rear of the casket. He came to attention, saluted the casket and remained frozen in position as it was slowly lowered into the ground.

Mike and Sandy remained in their seats facing the burial site holding hands tightly. She cradled the folded flag to her breast like a small child. Both wept openly for several minutes as the others began to slowly wander back to their cars parked along the road. A few friends and relatives bent down to whisper condolences but most left them alone in their grief. An Army chaplain, a Major Keene, came over to them to offer his condolences and to remind them that the Army provided grief counseling for the next of kin. With a double chin that wobbled when he talked and wearing a uniform that he had outgrown, Mike thought he looked like a country bumpkin. Two representatives from the mortuary stood quietly off to the side of the burial site waiting patiently. A light rain had blown in from the gray skies but went unnoticed. Eventually they stood, looked around the site noticing that most had departed, and then walked slowly back to the hearse. Mike held Sandy securely around the waist fearing she would collapse.

They had decided not to invite others back to the house for the usual buffet, drinks and conversation. Neither felt like socializing. There was something so terrible about losing a child, something so unnatural, so heartbreaking, that they weren't ready to share their thoughts or feelings or even quiet time with anyone. No, it was a private evening of just going through the motions and reminding each other how nice the military ceremony was. They stayed up late to watch the TV news at ten and again at eleven wondering if the graveside ceremony had been captured by the media, but it was nothing but a woman trapped in a car accident on the freeway, a city council argument about misuse of the general fund for personal office renovations, and some high school student making stuffed animals for kids with cancer. Rain was expected for the next couple days.

Before getting ready for bed, Sandy walked into Patrick's room and looked around at his things. His football helmet on the shelf, a picture of his first prom date taped on his mirror, the heavy metal band posters on the walls, and the eight by eleven color photo of him leaning casually against the front fender of his red Mustang. His first car that he'd loved so much. Within a minute she had collapsed on the bed and begun moaning. Mike charged in thinking she had fallen but soon joined her in unabashed weeping, holding her tight. Neither said anything. They lay together on his bed for half an hour before moving to their own bedroom. Both tossed constantly through a sleepless night. Grief had elbowed its way in as a new member of the Casey family.

It was just a short article in the "Military Briefs" section of the newspaper the day after the funeral.

> The funeral of Army Infantryman Patrick Casey was held with full military honors at the Veterans' Cemetery yesterday morning. Casey, 21, a graduate of Springfield High School, was killed in an ambush in Iraq last week. He was a machine gunner assigned to the 5th Stryker Brigade of the 2nd Infantry Division at Ft. Lewis, WA. Casey is survived by his parents, Mike and Sandra Casey, of the Ridgeview Estates.

Mike read the article twice and slid it over the table to Sandy. "Didn't even include his picture," he snorted.

Sandy pushed her coffee aside and read the article closely. "Do you think the Army will give us a copy of the report? I mean, of what actually happened?"

"You mean like an after action report? I doubt it. Seems like killed in action is about all they figure we need. What else is there? He was out on patrol, they got ambushed, and he got killed. Here's the body. Thanks for his service. What's to know? That he was the four thousand three hundred and forty ninth American killed in Operation Iraqi Freedom?"

"Well, you don't have to be so callous about it. I mean, you're the one who encouraged his enlistment."

"Me? We both agreed that if that's what he wanted to do, we'd support his decision. Right?"

"Well, seems to me you were the one who suggested the Army in the first place. After the police department rejected him."

"C'mon Sandy, he was drifting. He didn't know what he wanted to do. And I thought the Army would give him a chance to grow up a bit and give him some time to make some decisions about what he wanted in life. The police department was just one of his options. I was never sure he wanted to be a cop anyway."

"You mean you were never sure he wanted to be like you and you resented that."

"Stop it, Sandy. This isn't about me. It's about Pat."

"And now he's gone." Tears welled up in her eyes. "I guess we can't help asking why. Now that he's gone."

"He was a great kid, and he died for his country. He was a patriot, Sandy, and I'm proud of him."

"Proud? Of what? Proud of him dying?"

"Serving his country. Sandy, he's gone but we gotta get over it."

"Get over it? How do you get over losing your only child?"

"Well, we're just going to have to accept it and move on."

"I just can't help thinking of how much he could have done, what he could have become, instead of being a machine gunner in the stupid army. I mean . . ."

"He sacrificed his life for others, Sandy, for his country. There's a special honor in that. And don't begrudge him for being a machine gunner. He had no choice about that."

She sighed. "Oh, it just seems such a waste. He was such a beautiful young man. Taken from us so quickly, and so violently. He never had the opportunity to be a proud husband, to father a child. And he died in that godforsaken country, where the people hate us and want us to leave. And for what? They don't care about freedom, or democracy. What did they have to do with 9-11, anyway? It's just all so . . . . worthless."

"OK", Mike shot back. "Look, I'm not going to get into a political argument with you. He died a hero and no one can dispute that." He got up and stomped out of the kitchen.

Mike took a couple weeks off from the department and hung around the house with Sandy, but eventually her moping around got through to him. It was depressing. One morning he put the newspaper down at breakfast and announced that he had decided to go back to work. She took it well, saying she understood and thought it would be good for him to get busy with something else. They continued to debate their positions on the death of Patrick though. Mike persisted that he died a hero and encouraged Sandy to accept the loss and to get on with her life. He suggested they remodel Patrick's room and turn it into a workroom for her projects. But Sandy refused, insisting that his room remain just how he left it expecting to return; that it remain a kind of shrine to him. They grieved, but it was grief unshared.

Mike turned his frustration into physical exercise and joined a cycling club which took him out into long rides on the weekends, pounding his grief into the roads. Sandy would sit alone in Patrick's room, fondling his memorabilia and massaging her memories. Her hurt had turned physical. Every bone in her body ached. Many days she rarely got out of bed, dozing off, weeping, playing with the memories over and over, uncaring that her physical strength withered. Everything hurt. All too often there seemed to be no reason to keep on living.

Privately, each yearned for an acceptance and a peace which remained elusive and never seemed to come.

It was on a Tuesday night, shortly after dinner as she was loading the dish washer and Mike had retreated to his home office to read his mail and pay some bills when the phone rang.

"Mrs. Casey?" The line sounded hollow, with a slight echo to it.

"Yes."

"This is Captain Derrick Hunter, from the 5th Stryker Brigade, 2nd Infantry Division, U.S. Army."

Sandy's mind froze.

"Ma'am, your son Patrick was a team leader assigned to my company in Iraq."

Sandy groped around for a chair to collapse in. "Patrick. Yes, my son", her voice faltered.

"I wanted to call you and tell you about Patrick."

"Yes, please, wait, let me get my husband." She put the phone down and yelled, "Mike, it's Patrick's captain on the phone."

Mike picked up the phone in his office, "This is Mike Casey".

"Sir, this is Captain Derrick Hunter, and I'm calling about your son, Patrick".

Sandy listened on the other line in the kitchen. "Go ahead, captain", said Mike.

"Well, I make it a practice to write or call the families of all my soldiers who have been injured" . . . , he hesitated, "or killed in action, and I want to tell you that Patrick was a good soldier. He carried out his assignments in an exemplary manner and was greatly respected by his fellow soldiers and his superiors." He sounded like he was reading from an annual performance report.

Sandy smiled at the description. "Patrick loved the Army, captain. He wrote us that he felt we were winning the war on terrorism."

Mike frowned.

The captain continued on, "Yes, well, it was extremely unfortunate that his squad suffered so many injuries and deaths. Patrick had led his team into a ravine in search of a small group of insurgents when they opened fire on them from heavily fortified positions. Within minutes most of his squad had been injured or killed."

Mike sat up and became more interested. "Didn't they have time to call for help, or a rescue?"

"Well, yes sir, they . . ." the captain started.

"What about air support? Isn't that what the helicopters are for? The Apaches and the Blackhawks that Patrick talked about. What about the drones?"

"Well, actually they did, sir. But because of their proximity to a local village that response had to be delayed before approving a fire mission. They held out for almost an hour before most of the squad succumbed to injury and death. We weren't able to recover all of them until the following day."

"Captain." Mike stood up. "Are you telling me that my son died because the Army was more afraid of injuring civilians than protecting its soldiers?"

The captain hesitated, "No, sir, I don't think I could say that, but it's not uncommon for a fire mission request to take awhile to obtain clearance."

"So it's about the rules of engagement then", suggested Mike.

"Well, the rules of engagement do become an issue sometimes. Yes, sir."

Mike persisted. "But air support or an artillery fire mission could have saved their lives, right?"

"Well, it would have been helpful", the captain winced on the other end of the line, realizing that this was getting complicated.

"Did they radio for help? For reinforcements?"

"We're still in the process of determining what happened, sir, and we don't have all the facts yet, or the report of investigation. When we do, we'll have a better picture of what actually occurred." He realized he was being dragged into something he had hoped to avoid.

Sandy listened wide-eyed.

Mike took a deep breath. "So what I've read is true. The Army is being driven by politics. Being politically correct. Saving the lives of civilians in that worthless country is more important than saving the lives of our own soldiers. Is that a correct statement, captain?"

"Now Mike, please don't . . . ." Sandy started, but was interrupted by Mike.

"No, be quiet Sandy. Go ahead captain. Answer the question. Those sanctimonious bastards in Washington are running that war, aren't they?"

"Mr. and Mrs. Casey, I just wanted to tell you", the captain tried to wrap it up, "That your son was a good man and a brave and courageous soldier. He died protecting his fellow soldiers, and he died for his country. I've made a recommendation that he be awarded the Army Commendation Medal with a V for his bravery. You have my condolences on his death. The Department of the Army should be sending you an official cause of death report in a few months. You'll need that for some of his insurance documents."

Mike felt the captain trying to escape.

"Were mistakes made, captain?"

"Sir, that's something I'm not qualified to answer. The investigation will focus and report on the planning, risk assessment, tactical actions and command decisions made during the engagement. But sometimes in the fog of war . . ." he was cut off by Mike.

"Engagement! You mean the death of my son."

"Sir . . ."

"And will someone be disciplined if they are found to be in error, or incompetent—resulting in the death of my son?"

"Sir, I just can't answer that. You'll have to wait for the Report of Investigation which will be produced in strict accordance with Section 6 of Army Regulation 15."

"I don't give a damn about what section of army regulations will be used to produce a report. I want to know what happened to my son."

"Of course, sir."

"And just when will this report of investigation be made available to my wife and me, captain?"

"That's hard to say, sir, probably within a few months."

Mike shook his head silently. He had a bad feeling about how this was going to end.

"OK, well, thank you for calling, captain, we appreciate your efforts", he said slowly. "Sorry I got a bit riled up, there. I'm sure you can understand what an emotional experience this is for us."

"No problem, sir, I understand. I'm glad I had an opportunity to talk to you." The line went to a dial tone.

Mike clicked the phone off and sat down in his chair. Sandy placed her phone into the wall cradle carefully, as if it were something valuable or precious, and walked into Mike's office. It was obvious that she had been crying.

"Well, at least we know more than before", said Mike, shaking his head. "Patrick died in a ditch because the Army was afraid of injuring someone in that goddam village. A hostile village. I'll promise you one thing, honey; I've read enough after action reports to recognize a whitewash. And they're not going to get away with writing off Patrick's death to cover their ass. If somebody fucked up, they're going to read about it and they're going to pay for it. Patrick deserves that."

He stood up, walked over to Sandy and embraced her like she thought he had forgotten.

A month later they received an invitation from the local Army base to join a counseling group for parents who had experienced the loss of a military child.

"Well, why not?" asked Sandy, showing the invitation to Mike.

He glanced at it briefly and snorted. "This is just the military version of Dr. Phil. They're looking for couples who will blow up like on TV and throw things at each other. It's just entertainment. I don't believe in shrinks anyway. I don't need some stranger to tell me how to get over Patrick's death."

Sandy frowned at him but said nothing. She knew when it was better not to push. Since the captain's phone call he'd been granted an indefinite leave of absence from the police department and he'd been cooped up in his office researching the incident. She had also accepted his absences while biking on the weekends, but she'd noticed he'd been drinking more lately also. And she had fallen back on her own anti-depressants. They were both fighting demons, drifting apart, spending less and less time together. Mike usually wandered back into his office or the garage after dinner and became involved in some kind of project which kept them apart until bedtime. Whether it was deliberate or unintentional made no difference to Sandy. Regardless, it kept them apart. Their conversations had become short and devoid of real interest in each other. Functional instead of engaging, like roommates or siblings. They had sex a couple times since the funeral but both were unsatisfying for Sandy which only made Mike feel selfish and demanding. He felt like a failure when it came to compassion and loving. And so he pulled away. The looks, the touching, the affection stopped. Their love was slowly dying like the late night embers of a campfire and neither seemed interested in rekindling it.

She held off a couple more months before she brought up the subject of counseling again. This time she waited until after he'd had a drink and dinner before bringing it up.

"Mike, we received another invite from the base for family counseling. I think we ought to re-consider this," she paused. "It may be helpful. We don't have to keep going if you don't like it", she suggested hopefully.

He looked at her suspiciously. "Really?"

"Yes, I really do. I think it's worth a try."

He hesitated, and took a sip of his drink. "OK, just once, to check it out. Then we're out of there." He held up his glass and gave her a nod.

The four couples sat in a semi-circle with the psychologist, Dr. Altman. They had introduced themselves, and then shared and described the loss of their military child. Some had talked mechanically as if it had happened to someone else or they'd watched a TV program, and others had broken down, weeping, mumbling, struggling to get it out. Sandy had gamely participated, broke down several times, of course, but finally got through it. When it came to Mike's turn he refused saying he just wasn't ready to discuss his feelings with the group. Dr. Altman probed gently but Mike refused and shutdown. He wasn't about to lose his cool in front of this audience, thought Sandy.

There was a great deal of discussion about the stages of the grieving process and how each individual differs in coping style. The psychologist discussed the use of drugs to fight depression, the common misuse of alcohol, and the benefit of having someone to talk to; the "why me, why our son or daughter." The frustration of dealing with unresolved issues. Problems dealing with the Army organization. He also suggested one on one counseling for the couples with a therapist.

Sandy took notes. Mike fought to stay awake.

At the end of the session, the psychologist asked how many couples would like to return. Sandy raised her hand, and then looked at Mike, who shrugged.

Neither said anything on the ride home. Sandy thought about continuing the dialogue Dr. Altman had suggested about how parents see things differently. Mike thought about having a couple shots of Jim Beam as a reward for attending the counseling session.

They met with the group on two more occasions before Mike reluctantly agreed to a session with just him and Sandy. He hadn't participated much in the group sessions but with Sandy's gentle pushing he had finally given in. He had made it clear that he expected nothing from the session and that he was only going along to make Sandy happy. It was so Mike, she thought. He was too proud to accept help from anyone.

"So, my good friends, how are we tonight?" Dr. Altman opened with a toothy grin. The John Lennon glasses he wore as a tribute to his survival of the '60's magnified his blue eyes. He can't wait to pry into our personal lives, thought Mike. He also thought his pointy little beard was prissy.

Neither answered.

"So, would you like to talk about what you expect from our session today, or maybe why you are here? Other than the obvious, of course. What would you prefer?"

Sandy looked at Mike who stared straight ahead.

"C'mon, now folks", he laughed. "I have to hear from one of you."

Sandy shifted in her seat uncomfortably. "Well, obviously losing our son has created problems. For both of us, and I think it has significantly affected our relationship." She looked quickly at Mike who returned her glance. "And I'm hoping that maybe counseling can help us."

She looked at Mike. "Don't you think, Mike?"

He looked directly at her and then at the psychologist. "Yeah, maybe".

Dr. Altman turned his attention to Mike. "Is that what you are expecting also, Mike?"

"Yeah", he paused, "It's been tough for both of us."

"Would you like to describe how your relationship has been affected?"

"Well, I guess so." Mike mumbled. "Sandy says we're just not communicating."

"And drifting apart", Sandy added quickly. "You just hang out in your office and the garage and don't talk to me anymore. And off riding your bike on the weekends. It's like I'm not there anymore."

"Oh you're there all right. Crying all day in the bedroom. I'm just sick of it. You gotta get over it, Sandy. Life goes on."

Dr. Altman looked from one to the other. "So you think there should be more discussion between the two of you?"

"We just seem to be living separate lives", Sandy said looking to Mike for agreement.

"And we don't even talk about Patrick anymore."

Dr. Altman turned to Mike. "Do you feel that way Mike?"

Instantly, he felt cornered. "No, I really don't, and I don't know where Sandy gets that." He turned to her. "We talk about Patrick all the time."

The doctor looked at Mike. "Everyone deals with grief differently. We've discussed that previously in group. Maybe you're compartmentalizing your grief, Mike, and not sharing with Sandy. Do you share personal issues easily with her?"

Sandy laughed. "Doctor, Mike hardly shares feelings with anyone. He did tell me he loved me once, though. At our wedding."

"Now dammit, Sandy", Mike shot back, "Don't start that shit again."

"Mike, when is the last time you told me you loved me? Huh? You can't remember, can you, because I can't either."

The doctor listened quietly.

"Look", Mike started, "Maybe I'm not as emotional as you, and I don't mope around all day, crying, carrying Patrick's photo in my pocket. Wishing he'd walk in the front door. Well, it ain't gonna happen, Sandy. He's dead. It's terrible, and we both miss him terribly. But we've got to get on with our lives, and get past this thing."

"Get past this thing? Patrick's death is just a THING?"

"You know I didn't mean it that way. C'mon, Sandy."

"That's what I don't understand about you, Mike. You treat Patrick's death so mechanically, so matter of fact. Almost like he was someone else's son. Well, he wasn't. He was ours, and now he's gone and God, I miss him so much, and . . ." she began to cry.

Dr. Altman waited a minute, expecting Mike to console Sandy. Instead he sat quietly watching her cry.

"Mike", the doctor began, "Do you feel that Sandy's criticism is fair?"

It went on for another ten minutes but only grew more heated. Suddenly Mike stood up.

"OK, we're out of here. Let's go Sandy. I've had enough of this bullshit for the day." He stalked out of the office and slammed the door.

Sandy stood up slowly, wiping her eyes with a tissue and shrugged at the doctor. "I'll call your secretary later to schedule another appointment when Mike feels better."

He smiled, patted her on the shoulder and walked her to the door. After he closed it he went over to the window overlooking the parking lot and watched her walk over to the car where Mike was waiting. He said something to her which made her to take a step back and shake her head. A minute later they were gone. Altman sat down at his desk, hesitated, and then wrote a note in their file. He doubted he would see them again.

S everal months later Sandy received a telephone call from Harold Chambers, who said he had been in Patrick's platoon, that he was on leave and in town, and that he'd like to stop by and meet Pat's parents. Was Friday night okay? She had immediately agreed, even though Patrick had never mentioned a Harold Chambers or written about him, but she was terribly curious and hopeful that he could tell them something about Patrick. Mike seemed just as anxious to meet Harold saying he hoped he might be able to tell them more about the firefight.

They waited anxiously for Friday not knowing what to expect.

And then on Friday night a few minutes after five Harold Chambers arrived, standing at the front door, wearing his Army uniform. The reality of who he was and why he was there was like a slap in the face for Sandy. It was also a replay of the visit by the uniformed death notification officers several months before. Nervously, she invited him in, made him comfortable in the living room and offered him something to drink, although she couldn't stop staring at the red and black snake tattoo curled around the side of his neck poking out of his shirt collar.

"Why, ma'am, I'd love a cold beer, if you have one", he grinned kind of stupidly.

"Of course, Harold", Sandy said as if he were an old friend, and she brought both Harold and Mike a cold Coors.

"So where are you from, Harold?" asked Mike, trying to get started.

"Mississippi, sir. Tupelo. Up in the northeast corner of the state."

"Ah, yes. Elvis Presley was from Tupelo, wasn't he? He was a truck driver up there, wasn't he? Before he started singing."

"Yes, sir. He's kinda like one of our local heroes. He's been gone a long time, though. Moved over to Memphis and built a great big house. We never knew his family, if yer wonderin' if we was friends or somethin'."

Mike smiled and wondered how in the world his son Patrick and Harold could possibly have been friends.

Harold took another sip of his beer and fussed with his hat which he had folded and slipped under the epaulet on his left shoulder. Mike noticed that he had three rows of ribbons above the left pocket of his uniform. He wondered what they were for but didn't ask.

"We got us a lot of gamblin' casinos up around Tupelo now. A bunch of Indians claimed some of the land was hallowed or somethin', built the casinos, and became millionaires overnight. People hate 'em but they keep going to the casinos so I figure they don't hate 'em that much," he laughed to himself. "Almost makes ya wanna be an Indian, if you know what I mean."

Amazingly insightful of you Harold, thought Mike. "So tell me about Patrick", he asked, fishing for anything.

"Well, he was one cool dude, ya know", Harold laughed as he powered down half the beer. "We all liked Pat. And he was one mean mutha . . ."

he paused," . . . I mean awesome, with a machine gun. He'd just laugh pickin' off them hajjis with that machine gun."

Harold looked at the bottle and smiled to himself remembering something that he didn't share.

Mike glanced at Sandy and raised an eyebrow.

"He was well liked in the platoon, ya know, and he was one helluva gamer."

"A gamer?" asked Sandy.

"Yeah, video gamer. You know. War games. He was the best in the platoon."

Sandy shook her head wondering how her sweet little Patrick could have turned into a war games freak.

Harold continued, "And his loss was a pretty tough thing for the guys, if ya know what I mean. He was a good team leader. Real good with the younger guys."

Younger guys? Thought Mike. Patrick was only twenty one.

"And he was also real proud of being an American", Harold became more animated.

"One of the FNG's, that's, ah," he paused, "one of the new guys, had bought a cigarette lighter with the twin towers engraved on it at the local marketplace and when Pat saw it he told him to get rid of it or he'd shove it up . . . well, anyway, Pat went down to the market the next day and found this hajji who had sold him the lighter and beat the shit outa him. Trashed his sales stand. Yeah, he was a real patriot, Pat was."

Sandy looked over at Mike beginning to think inviting Harold over may have been a mistake.

He went on for awhile talking about the sandstorms, the women hiding inside their robes in public and how hot it got during the summer. "Too hot for a white man", he laughed loudly.

It took Mike several minutes and another beer to bring Harold around to the firefight when Patrick had been killed.

"So, what happened that day, Harold, when Patrick was killed?"

"Well sir, we been chasing some hajjis outside this village. We'd taken fire from the village, and we chased them down into a ravine. And they had set up an ambush. Jesus, it was bad." He paused, drained most of his beer and hunched forward a little bit more.

Mike and Sandy watched him intently, waiting, not wanting to push to hard.

"And then, all of a sudden, they just opened up on us, and all hell broke loose."

"And that's when Patrick was hit?" Mike asked impatiently.

"No sir, not at first."

"But you radioed for help," interrupted Mike.

"Yes sir, after awhile, but it never came. We was too close to the village. So we jus hunkered down and did our best but we kept taking incoming small arms fire, you know. B-40 rockets and mortars too. Them mortars really done the job on us."

"So that's when Patrick was hit?" asked Mike.

"Yes sir, he hung on for a long time though, he'd been hit a couple times, but he hung in there until he finally . . . passed. It was awful." He motioned with the beer and Sandy got up to get him another one.

"So where was the air support?" asked Mike.

"Dunno, sir. They was 'afraid of injuring civilian Iraqis, I guess. We were too close to the village."

"But you said the village had fired on you, right?" Mike reminded him.

"Yessir."

"So there were enemy troops in the village?"

"Yeah, I guess so. Musta been."

"And they still denied the air support?"

"Yessir", he slurred his answer this time.

"And you requested a fire support mission, and they denied artillery also?"

"I think so. I think the sergeant called it in. Maybe not. I'm not sure about anything anymore, sir. It was pretty intense."

"So Patrick was hit by small arms fire?"

"Well, I think so. Or shrapnel from the mortars. When the rest of the platoon arrived, some of the guys separated and went up the hill to flank the hajjis. Later we thought maybe they was the ones shootin' at us, but we weren't sure."

"Your own guys were shooting at you?" Mike was almost screaming at him by now.

"I don't know, sir. I'm sorry. The whole place turned to shit real fast, you know. Guys bleedin' and screamin' and lying all over the ravine."

Mike looked over at Sandy who was trying to keep from breaking down. Tears poured down her cheeks and her lips quivered.

"It was pretty trippy, if you know what I mean. Ya know, it was pretty bad. And I'm here to tell ya I've had some pretty intense nightmares myself. Yes sir, I do indeed. Some pretty bad things happened down there in that ravine" . . . his voice died. "Things I don't want to remember".

Mike noticed that Harold was three beers down.

"Are you saying that Patrick might have been killed by his fellow soldiers? By friendly fire?" asked Mike with a disturbing growl in his voice. Sandy looked at him.

"I ain't saying nothing, Mr. Casey. I'm jus' saying it was a pretty bad scene out there. In that ravine. I don't think . . . maybe nobody knows . . . what really happened out there. It's still under investigation, I guess."

He leaned down, eyes on the floor, and Mike decided that was the end of the beer.

"Look, Harold, I think maybe you ought to be going."

"Sure, look, thanks, I just thought I'd stop by and tell y'all that Patrick was a good troop and a great guy and we're gonna miss him . . . and . . ." he trickled out of words.

Mike walked him out the door, thanked him for coming, and watched him stagger down the steps to his rented Ford Focus. He walked back into the house and sat down in front of Sandy who trying to put herself back together. He took her hands in his.

"Jesus. Could that knucklehead be right? Was Patrick the victim of friendly fire? Or the victim of American politics?"

Sandy looked back at him. "Does it really matter, Mike? He's gone. Nothing is going to change that."

"Sandy, that Mississippi redneck has just blown this cover-up wide open!"

The next morning Sandy found Mike in his office composing a letter to the Department of the Army.

"I've got to know the truth", he said.

Within months Mike had turned his office into a production room of form letters, faxes, Army organizational charts, lists of political representatives, maps, and military investigative manuals. There were letters to write, letters to read, letters to categorize, letters to review for additional leads, letters to respond to letters. Any one of them could have held the answer and Mike left nothing unread. He hired a retired police sergeant from the department to track down and interview the survivors of the ambush; and he hired an attorney with military law experience to navigate through the morass of military regulations. He wanted to force Captain Hunter and Patrick's platoon leader to provide sworn statements. Of special interest was identifying those in the fire mission control center who refused the request for air or artillery support. He requested a copy of Patrick's military personnel records file from the NPRC in Saint Louis, Missouri and copies of the organizational history of the 5th Stryker Brigade.

He wrote the Director of the FBI under the auspices of the Freedom of Information Act and demanded an investigation into the Army conspiracy and obstruction of justice to deny the parents of a soldier the full story of their son's KIA death. He wrote the county District Attorney's office and demanded an investigation into the death of Patrick, one of his constituents. He wrote to every member of the House Military Affairs Committee and each member of the Foreign Affairs Committee. He demanded answers from his state Senators and Congressmen so often that he was on a first name basis with their staff. Mike Casey was relentless.

He researched the Pat Tillman case and the Army cover-up of the conclusions of the investigation for parallels and helpful investigative suggestions. He had turned his home office into a command post of investigation. He slept on the couch in his office many nights awaiting a call from back east because of the time differential. The three months turned into four, then six. His return to the department had become questionable, but no longer important to him. He had become addicted. Nothing was more important than his search for the truth.

Unnoticed by Mike, Sandy had begun to develop her own world. She had started a support group for mothers and wives at the base and was on the verge of forming several other groups nationwide which had drawn the interest of the media. She was attractive, articulate and sympathetic. TV and radio interviews, speaking at various women's' forums, and building her support network nationally had begun to demand all of her waking hours. It seemed she was traveling two to three weeks a month, much of it by herself. It had begun to consume her.

It was a quiet Wednesday evening, a typical night out bowling for so many of the locals, when Sandy had come home from a late meeting. Mike had wandered out of his office to scrounge through the refrigerator for something that hadn't spoiled. He sniffed a container of Chinese, flipped it into the trash and continued to rummage around for something edible. He finally found a hot dog, examined it carefully for anything green and then held it under the hot water in the sink for a minute before taking a bite.

Sandy poured herself a glass of merlot and sat down at the kitchen table.

"Mike. Do you know what today is?" she asked.

He spun around and looked at her. "Huh?"

"This is the anniversary of Patrick's death."

He winced and then collapsed into one of the other chairs. "Jesus. How could we possibly have forgotten?"

"We?" Sandy snorted.

"Look, I'm sorry . . ." he started before being interrupted.

"It's not about him anymore, Mike. It's about you. You may have found a way to survive, your own way of coping. But now it's without him. Without his memory. You've become so selfish you've forgotten Patrick. Look at you, Mike. Three days beard. You haven't changed clothes in days. You come out of that cave only to check the mail and to forage for food. You've become obsessed, no, addicted, to that goddamn investigation. We've become roommates, not a married couple. We're not important to each other anymore. We have separate lives and we don't need each other anymore."

"What do you mean, Sandy?" Mike was starting to realize the implications of what she was saying.

"You know that saying, 'You complete my life'. Well, you don't. I don't need you anymore."

"Sandy. You don't mean that. Don't . . ."

"I'm leaving Mike," she interrupted. "I can't live like this. There is no point for us to act like we're a married couple anymore."

"What do you mean, you're leaving?"

"I'm leaving. I've rented a small condo on the west side and I'm going to move out this weekend. It's fully furnished, so you can have everything here in the house. I don't need or want anything. I'll write checks out of the house account, and continue to use the credit cards which I'm sure you don't mind. It could be worse. I could ask for more. And you'd lose, of course. But I'm not interested in bankrupting you. I just need to get away from you."

"You can't do that. Why are you doing this?" He stood up confrontationally. "Is there someone else?"

"No, I'm just leaving you. I have other friends, but there isn't another man. There is no affair. I'm just re-starting my life again. Without you."

"Are you filing for a divorce?"

"No. Not yet. It doesn't seem necessary right now. I just need to get away from you and all your bullshit about the truth surrounding Patrick's death. The truth doesn't matter to me anymore. Whether it was the fault of his platoon leader, a colonel in the fire mission center, or the fucking Secretary of Defense himself. It doesn't matter. It's not going to change the fact that Patrick is dead. He's gone. And who's responsible is just not important. It isn't. I don't care anymore. I just have to get away from your insanity. I'm moving on."

Mike looked at her incredulously. He never saw it coming. Of course he didn't. He had become too myopic to see anything but his quest for the truth. For the last year he had been looking at life through the sights of a gun aimed at the United States Army and anyone else who stepped in front of him and his aim never faltered. He was hell bent on vengeance. Someone had to pay and he was going to find that someone. It had begun to eat away at his guts like a metastasizing cancer. It ravaged his soul. Mike Casey was a sick and broken man.

"I've scheduled a moving company to come over on Saturday to pick up a few of my things. Promise me you won't interfere with them, Mike. I'm going over to Marie's for a couple nights and you can do whatever. I'll be OK. I'm sorry, Mike. I loved you. But the Mike I loved died a year ago. Just like Patrick. My two loves. I'm broken too, Mike, but I can see it. I realize it. Which is something you don't. You have no idea that you've gone mad."

She drained the glass of merlot and stood up. "I'm sorry Mike. It's over." She gave him a tender kiss on the cheek, found her purse and turned around to leave.

She pulled the door shut without Mike getting up from his chair. He sat silently and listened to the sound of her car pulling out of the driveway. After a few minutes he slowly padded back to his office. He shuffled through the mail and then picked up an unopened letter from the Associate Deputy to the Under Secretary of Defense of the United States.

He opened it carefully and began reading. Maybe, he thought, just maybe . . .